S0-BLN-222

For current pricing information,
or to learn more about this or any Nextext title,
call us toll-free at **1-800-323-5435**
or visit our web site at www.nextext.com.

A CLASSIC RETELLING

The Tales of
O. Henry

nextext

Printed in the United States of America
ISBN 0-618-08596-3

4 5 6 7 — QVK — 06 05 04

Picture Acknowledgements

6 © THE GRANGER COLLECTION, New York

7 © THE GRANGER COLLECTION

8 © North Wind Picture Archives

12 © North Wind Picture Archives

13 "Eating By Machinery" by Charles Grunwald, from *Harper's Weekly*, 1903.
Library of Congress, Washington D.C.

14 Sam DeVincent Collection of Illustrated American Sheet Music, Archives
Center, Museum of American History, Smithsonian Institution.

Table of Contents

PART I: THE BIG CITY

In this famous story, a poor young couple wonders and worries about what to give each other for Christmas. The gifts they decide on— and how they buy them—show the depth of their love and generosity.

A homeless man named Soapy is looking for a place to spend the winter months. He decides that the most comfortable place is jail. But how can he get himself arrested?

*Vocabulary words appear in boldface type and are
footnoted. Specialized or technical words and phrases
appear in lightface type and are footnoted.*

William Sidney Porter

Background

O. Henry

O. Henry is the pen name of William Sidney Porter. Some critics say he is one of the greatest short story writers in American history.

Porter was born in Greensboro, North Carolina, on September 11, 1862. As a young man, he worked for five years in his uncle's drugstore, filling prescriptions. Porter tired of the pharmacy, however, and drifted off to Texas. There he worked at a ranch and later as a bank teller. He also tried his hand at writing. In 1887, Porter married seventeen-year-old Athol Estes, the daughter of a wealthy Austin, Texas, businessman.

The period from 1887 to 1891 was the happiest time in Porter's life. He and his young wife found a tiny set of rooms to rent and began thinking about starting a family. With his wife's

Young Porter worked in his uncle's drugstore.

support, Porter began to write stories for national magazines. Athol probably was the model for Della in "The Gift of the Magi," his most famous work. But their happiness was short-lived. Porter's wife was diagnosed with tuberculosis. The death of their first child a few days after birth stunned the young couple. Their second child, a daughter named Margaret, was born a year later.

In 1894, Porter resigned his bank job to start a humorous weekly magazine called *The Rolling Stone*. When the magazine failed, he joined the *Houston Post* as a reporter, columnist, and cartoonist. To earn extra money, he also took a job as a bank teller. In 1896, Porter was accused of stealing money from the bank. Although he said

A thief steals money at a bank. Porter heard many stories from thieves in jail.

he was innocent, Porter went into hiding in Honduras, a country in Central America. There he met others who had also fled from the United States. Eventually, he would write about many of them in his articles and stories.

After a year in Central America, Porter learned that his beloved wife was dying. Desperate to see her one more time, Porter returned to the United States and was arrested. In 1897, Athol died. In 1898, Porter was sentenced to five years in a Columbus, Ohio, jail.

During his time in jail (from April 1898 to July 1901), Porter began to write in earnest, hoping to earn enough money to support his young daughter. Because he didn't want readers to know that he was in prison, he used the pen name of O. Henry.

Writing as O. Henry, Porter published twelve or more stories during this period. The characters in these and later stories were based on inmates he met or heard about while in jail. The most famous was Jimmy Connors, who appears as Jimmy Valentine in "A Retrieved Reformation," one of Porter's most popular stories.

After Porter was released from prison, he traveled to New York City and began writing full-time under the name O. Henry. Some of his most famous stories, including "The Gift of the Magi" and "The Last Leaf," are set in New York City. These stories and others earned him a reputation as a gifted storyteller. He had a remarkable talent for capturing both the beauty and the ugliness of New York City life. He was known in New York as a pleasant, kind man.

With each new story he published, Porter's popularity grew. Eventually, he had a following of loyal readers who eagerly anticipated each new O. Henry story. Despite his successes, however, Porter was never quite happy. Illness, poverty, and alcoholism made his final years unhappy ones. He died penniless and alone in 1910.

Time Line

1862—William Sidney Porter is born.

1883—Porter goes to Texas, where he works at a series of jobs and begins writing.

1887—He marries Athol Estes.

1896—Accused of stealing money from a bank, Porter flees to Central America. He returns to the United States when he hears that his wife is dying.

1897—Athol Porter dies.

1898—Porter is convicted and goes to jail. In prison, he begins writing under the pen name O. Henry.

1901—Porter is released from prison and wins acclaim as a short-story writer.

1904—*Cabbages and Kings*, a book of short stories set in Central America, is published.

1906—Porter writes "The Gift of the Magi" and "The Last Leaf." Both stories are instantly popular.

1908–1909—Several O. Henry short-story collections, including *The Voice of the City*, *The Gentle Grafter*, and *Roads of Destiny*, are published.

1910—Porter writes "The Ransom of Red Chief." Shortly afterward, he dies penniless and alone.

While in prison, Porter wrote to earn money for his young daughter.

Prison Life

William Sidney Porter spent more than three years in prison for the crime of embezzlement (stealing funds). Although his years in prison were clearly the most difficult of his life, Porter was able to use this time as a way to gather information for his stories. He met prisoners and heard about crimes that he found fascinating. He learned about men who were lifetime criminals and men who longed to reform themselves. His stories, written under the name of O. Henry, describe these people with humor or irony, but always with some degree of respect. Interestingly, Porter did not write about his own prison experiences, although many people urged him to do so. "I will forget that I ever breathed behind these walls," he said, shortly before he was set free. For the rest of his life, he stayed true to his promise and never once wrote or spoke about his years in prison.

O. Henry's New York City

Porter loved New York City. He was fascinated by the shops, the nightlife, and the bustle of the busy streets. He also loved the glamour. At the height of his popularity, Porter was able to dine in the fanciest

A café in New York City

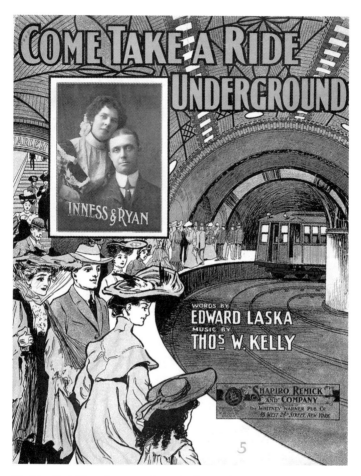

The New York City subway was the topic of a popular song.

restaurants and buy tickets for the most popular shows. Yet he never lost sight of the fact that there were thousands of men and women in the same city who were unable to do the same thing. He kept an eye on the "common folk" even when his life was a whirlwind of success.

Later, when his expensive tastes led to bankruptcy, Porter found himself among the common folk once again. Perhaps this is the reason he was able to write so effectively about both sides of New York City life. He had dined in the houses of the rich and had lived in the low-rent apartments of the working class and the poor. In many of his stories, Porter called New York City "Baghdad-on-the-Subway." He used this term to link modern New York in his readers' imaginations with the exotic settings of *The Arabian Nights*, a collection of romantic and magical stories set in ancient Baghdad, a city in Iraq.

Porter loved New York because it was exciting. But he also loved the city for another reason. In this huge city, with its hundreds of thousands of people, he felt safe at last. He stopped worrying that his past would catch up to him and certainly never told anyone about his time in jail. He built a reputation as O. Henry, and was able to leave William Sidney Porter behind him forever.

O. Henry's Stories

Story Structure

O. Henry's stories follow a pattern that looks like this.

O. Henry's Stories

"The arresting beginning."

(Exposition)

Reader's first guess about how things will turn out.

(Rising Action)

Reader discovers his or her guess is wrong.

(Climax)

The triumphant ending and sudden suspense.

(Falling Action)

The end of the story.

(Resolution)

Story Elements

O. Henry's stories were written to help people escape from their everyday problems. The author wanted them to be enjoyable. They have humor, irony, chance happenings, and surprise endings.

Humor and Irony

Some of O. Henry's stories are laugh-out-loud funny throughout (for example, "The Ransom of Red Chief"). Others deal with serious subject matter, and only include humor here and there. Most of the humor in O. Henry's stories takes the form of irony. When an author uses a word or phrase to mean the exact opposite of its literal or normal meaning, it is called "irony." Sometimes, the whole situation is ironic. The author sets up a scene one way, and then the opposite of what you might expect actually happens. An example is when Plumer, the homeless man in "A Madison Square Arabian Night," discovers that he must teach some manners to a wealthy and well-respected man. "The Gift of the Magi" contains a plot twist that is a classic example of irony. After you've read the story you'll really understand what "irony" means!

Coincidence

Coincidence (chance or luck) also plays a key role in most of O. Henry's stories. Very often the strange coincidences that the characters experience add another element of humor to the story. For example, in "After Twenty Years," two old friends make a plan to meet. But one has just learned something about the other, and this leads to an unexpected event. In "A Retrieved Reformation," it is a coincidence that Ben Price happens to be watching at the exact moment that Jimmy decides to save a little girl. In these stories and others, the coincidence acts as a kind of warm-up to the story's surprise ending.

Surprise Endings

O. Henry's stories are well known for their surprise endings. A surprise at the end of the story can bring an enormous amount of pleasure to readers. The key to a surprise ending—and it is one that O. Henry mastered early on—is that it has to be believable. The reader has to be able to say, "I see how that happened, but I didn't expect it." Consider, for example, the surprise endings in "The Last Leaf" and "The Third Ingredient." These endings are probably not what you predicted, but the outcome is reasonable just the same. In other words, you can accept the ending of the stories as the mark of a good writer and know that O. Henry tricked you once again.

The Big City

The Gift of the Magi

In this famous story, a poor young couple wonders and worries about what to give each other for Christmas. The gifts they decide on—and how they buy them—show the depth of their love and generosity.

One dollar and eighty-seven cents. That was all she had. And sixty cents of it was in pennies. Della had saved this amount one cent at a time. It seemed like it had taken forever! All through the fall, she had bargained and pleaded with the butcher and the vegetable man to lower their prices on carrots, on potatoes, on stew meat, on everything! Some days she had bargained so hard that her cheeks burned with shame. But the money was hers now, here in her hand. Three times Della counted it. One dollar and eighty-seven cents. It was such a small amount!

What could she buy for one dollar and eighty-seven cents? And the next day would be Christmas.

There was nothing to do but throw herself down on the worn couch and cry. So Della did it.

While the mistress of the home is crying on the couch, dear friends, take a look at the home, a tiny furnished apartment that costs $8 per week. The apartment is a bit rundown, a bit bare, but it is clean and bright, because Della works hard to keep it so.

At the door of the apartment hangs a small card with the name "Mr. James Dillingham Young." James had added the "Dillingham" to the card when he was making the wonderful salary of $30 per week. Now that his pay had shrunk to $20, the letters of "Dillingham" looked **blurred**.[1] But whenever Mr. James Dillingham Young came home and reached his apartment, he was called "Jim" and greatly hugged by Mrs. James Dillingham Young, already introduced to you as Della. Which is all very good.

Della finished her cry and powdered her cheeks quickly. Then she stood looking dully out the window at a gray cat walking back and forth on a gray fence in a gray backyard. Tomorrow would be Christmas day, and she had only $1.87 to spend on Jim's present. She had been saving every penny she could for months, and this was all she had.

---

[1] **blurred**—smeared, smudged.

Twenty dollars a week doesn't go far. The household expenses had been greater than she thought they would be. They always are. Only $1.87 to buy a present for Jim. Her Jim. She had spent so many happy hours planning for something nice for him. Something fine and rare and handsome—something almost as nice and wonderful and valuable as her dear, dear husband.

The household expenses had been greater than she thought they would be. They always are.

There was a mirror between the windows of the room. Perhaps you have seen a mirror in an $8 apartment. A very thin and very active person, by moving this way and that, might be able to catch a quick glimpse of himself or herself. Della, who was very slender, had mastered the art of catching her reflection in this mirror.

Suddenly she whirled from the window and stood before the glass. Her eyes were shining brilliantly, but her face had lost its color. Rapidly, she pulled down her hair and let it fall to its full length.

Now, the James Dillingham Youngs had two possessions of which they were very, very proud. One was Jim's gold watch, which had been his father's and his grandfather's. The other was

Della's hair. If the queen of Sheba[2] lived in the apartment across the alley, Della would have let her hair hang out of the window to dry just to show Her Majesty that her long strands could outshine even the finest jewels. If King Solomon[3] had been the janitor of the building, with all his treasures piled up high in the basement, Jim would have pulled out his watch every time he passed, just to see the king pull at his beard from envy.

So now Della's beautiful hair fell about her, rippling and shining like a **cascade**[4] of brown waters. It reached below her knees and was thick enough to be a cape. And then she pulled it back up again, nervously and quickly. Once she paused for a moment and stood still while a tear or two splashed on the worn red carpet.

Della pulled on her old brown jacket and her old brown hat. With a whirl of her skirts and with the brilliant sparkle still in her eyes, she whisked out the door and down the stairs to the street.

---

[2] queen of Sheba—in the Bible, a beautiful queen who brought rich gifts to King Solomon when she came to test his wisdom.

[3] King Solomon—king of Israel in the 10th century B.C. He was thought to be very wise.

[4] **cascade**—waterfall.

After a few steps, she stopped at a sign that read: "Madame Sofronie. Hair Goods of All Kinds." Della ran up the steps and stood in the shop, breathing fast. Madame Sofronie, large and pale, stood in the center of the tiny room.

She found it at last. It surely had been made for Jim and no one else.

"Will you buy my hair?" asked Della.

"I buy hair," said Madame. "Take yer hat off and let's have a look at it."

Down rippled the brown cascade.

"Twenty dollars," said Madame, lifting the mass of hair with a practiced hand.

"Give it to me quick," said Della.

Oh, and the next two hours were so happy. Della could hardly breathe from running so hard. Della went from store to store to store looking for Jim's present.

She found it at last. It surely had been made for Jim and no one else. There was no other like it in any of the stores, and she had turned all of them inside out. It was a platinum[5] watch chain that was simple in design, but it was all the more beautiful because of its simplicity. As soon as she saw it, Della

---

[5] platinum—gray metal, more valuable than gold.

knew that it must be Jim's. It was just like him. Quietness and value—the description applied to both Jim and the watch chain. Twenty-one dollars it cost, and she hurried home with the 87 cents. With that chain on his watch, Jim could check the time in any company. Before, the watch hung from an old leather strap hooked to his pocket. Now the watch had a chain that was as wonderful as the watch itself.

When Della reached home, her happiness gave way to sense and reason. She got out her curling irons and lighted the gas stove and went to work repairing the damage made by generosity added to love, which is always a huge task, dear friends—a huge task. Within forty minutes, her head was covered with tiny, close-lying curls that made her look wonderfully like a little schoolboy. She looked at her reflection in the mirror long, carefully, and critically.

"If Jim doesn't kill me," she said to herself, "before he takes a second look at me, he'll say I look like a Coney Island chorus girl.[6] But what could I do—oh! what could I do with a dollar and eighty-seven cents?"

---

[6] Coney Island chorus girl—dancer or singer who worked at Coney Island, an amusement park and beach in South Brooklyn, New York City.

* * *

By 7 o'clock, the coffee was made and the frying-pan on the back of the stove was hot and ready to cook the little lamb chops.

Jim was never late. Della folded the watch chain in her hand and sat on the corner of the table near the door that he always entered. When she heard his step on the stairs, she turned white for just a moment. She had a habit of saying little silent prayers about the simplest everyday things, and now she whispered: "Please, God, make him think I am still pretty."

The door opened and Jim stepped in and closed it. He looked thin and very serious. Poor fellow, he was only twenty-two—and had the difficult job of feeding a family! He needed a new winter coat and he was without gloves.

Jim stepped inside the door, and then stood as still as a hunting dog at the first sniff of duck. His eyes were fixed upon Della, and there was an expression in them that she could not read, and it terrified her. It was not anger, nor surprise, nor disapproval, nor horror, nor any of the emotions that she had been prepared for. He simply stared at her carefully with that strange expression on his face.

Della wriggled off the table and ran to him.

"Jim, darling," she cried, "don't look at me that way. I had my hair cut off and sold it because I couldn't have lived through Christmas without giving you a present. It'll grow out again—you won't mind, will you? I just had to do it. My hair grows awfully fast. Say 'Merry Christmas!' Jim, and let's be happy. You don't know what a nice—what a beautiful, nice gift I bought for you."

"You say your hair is gone?" he said, almost stupidly.

"You've cut off your hair?" asked Jim, slowly, as if he could not understand what he was looking at.

"Cut it off and sold it," said Della. "Don't you like me just as well, anyhow? I'm me without my hair, aren't I?"

Jim looked about the room curiously.

"You say your hair is gone?" he said, almost stupidly.

"You don't have to look for it," said Della. "It's sold, I tell you—sold and gone, too. It's Christmas Eve, boy. Be good to me, for it went for you. Maybe the hairs of my head were numbered," she went on with a sudden serious sweetness, "but nobody could ever count my love for you. Shall I put the lamb chops on, Jim?"

All of a sudden, Jim awoke from his confusion. He pulled Della to him and folded her in his arms. For ten seconds, dear friends, let us look about the apartment and wait for the two to collect themselves.

A little later, Jim pulled a package from his coat pocket and threw it on the table.

"Don't make any mistake about me, Dell," he said. "There's no haircut or shave or shampoo that could make me like my girl any less. But if you'll unwrap that package, you may see why I was so confused."

Della tore at the package with white fingers. When she saw what was inside, she gave a happy scream of joy, and then—Oh! just as quickly, her scream turned to tears and wails, which made it necessary for Jim to once again take her in his arms.

For there in the package lay the combs—the set of combs, side and back, that Della had worshipped for so long in a Broadway window. Beautiful combs, pure tortoiseshell,[7] with jeweled rims—just the shade to wear in the beautiful vanished hair. They were expensive combs, she knew, and her heart had longed for them even though she had had no hope of owning them. And now they were hers,

---

[7] tortoiseshell—made from the yellow-and-brown shell of a tortoise, used for combs, barrettes, and so forth.

but the hair that would have held these lovely combs was gone.

But she hugged them to her bosom, and at length she was able to look up with dim eyes and a smile and say: "My hair grows so fast, Jim!"

And then Della leaped up like a little cat and cried, "Oh, oh!"

Jim had not yet seen his beautiful present. She held it out to him eagerly upon her open palm. The chain gleamed brightly, though not nearly as brightly as the woman who held it.

"Isn't it dandy,[8] Jim? I hunted all over town to find it. You'll have to look at the time a hundred times a day now. Give me your watch. I want to see how it looks on it."

Instead of obeying, Jim sat down hard on the couch and put his hands under the back of his head and smiled.

"Dell," said he, "let's put our Christmas presents away and keep 'em a while. They're too nice to use right now. I sold the watch to get the money to buy your combs. And now suppose you put the chops on."

The **magi**,[9] as you know, were wise men—wonderfully wise men—who brought gifts to the

---

[8] dandy—wonderful.

[9] **magi**—wise men who brought gifts for the baby Jesus.

Babe in the manger.[10] They invented the art of giving Christmas presents. Because they were wise, their gifts were no doubt wise ones, perhaps fully returnable in the event that someone else brought the same thing. And here I have **lamely**[11] related to you the simple story of two foolish children in an apartment who most unwisely sacrificed for each other the greatest treasures of their house. But in a last word to the wise of these days, let it be said that of all who give gifts, these two were the wisest. Of all who give and receive gifts, such as they[12] are wisest. Everywhere they are wisest. They are the magi.

THE END

---

[10] Babe in the manger—a reference to the Christian story of the birth of Jesus.

[11] **lamely**—weakly.

[12] such as they—people who are like Jim and Della.

The Cop and the Anthem

A homeless man named Soapy is looking for a place to spend the winter months. He decides that the most comfortable place is jail. But how can he get himself arrested?

On his bench in New York's Madison Square, Soapy moved uneasily. When wild geese honk high in the night sky, when women without fur coats grow kind to their husbands, and when Soapy moves uneasily on his bench in the park, you know for sure that winter is near at hand.

A dead leaf fell in Soapy's lap. That was Jack Frost's[1] card, he knew. Jack is kind to the regular

---

[1] Jack Frost's—winter's.

citizens of Madison Square and gives fair warning when he's on his way. So Soapy took this as a sign that it was time for him to find a place to stay for the winter. He was not a fussy winter guest, by any means. All he wanted was a warm place to sleep and a meal to eat every once in a while. In fact, he knew just the place: three months on the Island was what his soul needed.

Three months of free meals, bed, and friendly company, safe from the police and criminals—the Island could offer it all.

Three months of free meals, bed, and friendly company, safe from the police and criminals—the Island could offer it all. For years the **hospitable**[2] Blackwell's[3] had been his winter quarters. Just as his more fortunate fellow New Yorkers had bought their tickets to Palm Beach and the Riviera[4] each winter, so Soapy had made his **humble**[5] preparations for his annual trip to the Island.

And now the time had come. The night before, three Sunday newspapers that he had spread underneath his coat, around his ankles, and over

---

[2] **hospitable**—friendly to strangers.

[3] Blackwell's—a prison island in the East River, in New York City.

[4] Palm Beach and the Riviera—two famous winter vacation spots for the wealthy. Palm Beach is in Florida, and the Riviera is in France on the Mediterranean Sea.

[5] **humble**—simple, lowly.

his lap had failed to keep out the cold as he slept on his bench. So Soapy's mind was on the Island, and nowhere else. He **scorned**[6] the free meals and rooms given by various charities in the city. In Soapy's opinion, the law was kinder and easier to take than philanthropy.[7]

There were an endless number of charities that could offer Soapy free food and lodging. But Soapy was a proud man. To his way of thinking, gifts from charity wanted something in return, not in money but in shame of spirit. No bed was offered without a bath, for example. No loaf of bread was offered without all kinds of questions and advice. On the Island, however, a gentleman could keep his private business private. This is why Soapy liked to spend his winters there.

Once Soapy had decided to go to the Island, he had to find a way to get arrested. He certainly didn't want any unpleasantness. Soapy considered his choices. His favorite method of attracting attention from the police was to dine luxuriously[8] at some expensive restaurant, and then, after telling the

---

[6] **scorned**—rejected.

[7] philanthropy—charity.

[8] dine luxuriously—eat a dinner of good food and wine.

waiter that he had no money, be handed over quietly and without fuss to a policeman. A judge could do the rest, and then he'd be happily on his way to the Island.

Soapy left his bench and strolled out of the **square**.[9] He made his way up Broadway and stopped at a glittering café. Soapy had confidence in himself from the lowest button of his vest upward. He was clean, his coat was decent, and he had a neat, black tie that a lady missionary had given to him on Thanksgiving Day. If he could get to a table without attracting attention, he was sure he could carry out his plan. The part of him that would show above the table wouldn't raise any doubt in a waiter's mind. A plate of roasted duck, he thought to himself, would be just the thing, along with a bottle of Chablis,[10] then Camembert,[11] a cup of coffee, and a cigar. He wouldn't order anything truly expensive, because he didn't want the café manager to be too angry about his trick. He needed just enough to leave him filled and happy for the journey to his winter home.

But, as Soapy walked through the restaurant door, the headwaiter's eye fell upon his **frayed**[12]

---

[9] **square**—small park at the intersection of two streets and surrounded by buildings. Madison Square is a very fashionable area of New York City.

[10] Chablis—type of white wine.

[11] Camembert—soft cheese imported from France.

[12] **frayed**—torn, tattered.

pants and muddy shoes. Strong and ready hands turned him around and pushed him silently out toward the sidewalk before he had a chance to ask for a table.

Soapy turned off Broadway. He wouldn't get to the Island through eating well. He'd have to find another way to get himself arrested. At a corner of Sixth Avenue, Soapy found what he was looking for. A brightly-lit store with a large plate-glass window in front seemed the ideal place. Soapy picked up a rock and threw it through the glass. People came running around the corner, a policeman in the lead. Soapy stood still, with his hands in his pockets, and smiled at the sight of a policeman.

Men who smash windows do not stay at the scene to talk with police officers. They take to their heels and run.

"Where's the man that done that?" asked the officer, excitedly.

"Don't you think that I might have had something to do with it?" said Soapy, in a friendly way, as one who greets good luck.

The policeman's mind refused to accept Soapy even as a clue. Men who smash windows do not stay at the scene to talk with police officers. They take to their heels and run. The policeman saw a man halfway down the block running to chase a car. Waving his club, the policeman ran after the man. Soapy, with disgust in his heart, turned away. Twice he had come close to being arrested, and twice he had failed.

On the opposite side of the street was a simpler restaurant. Clearly it was a place for large appetites and thin wallets. Its dishes and **atmosphere**[13] were thick; its soup and napkins thin. In this place, Soapy's torn pants and muddy shoes wouldn't be noticed.

S̲oapy was shown to a table, where he ordered and then ate plates full of beefsteak, pancakes, doughnuts, and pie. When he was finished, he called the waiter over and explained that his pockets were empty. He didn't have a penny to pay for his meal.

"Now, get busy and call a cop," said Soapy. "And don't keep a gentleman waiting."

"No cop for you," said the waiter, with a voice like butter cakes and an eye like the cherry in a Manhattan cocktail.[14] "Hey, Con!" he called out to another waiter.

The two waiters pitched Soapy neatly on his left ear onto the uncaring sidewalk. Aching all over,

---

[13] **atmosphere**—air and mood of the place.

[14] Manhattan cocktail—alcoholic drink served with a cherry.

Soapy pulled himself up joint by joint and beat the dust from his clothes. Arrest seemed to be just a happy dream. The Island seemed very far away. A policeman who stood before a drug store two doors away laughed and walked down the street.

Five blocks Soapy traveled before his courage permitted him to try to be captured again. This time a perfect opportunity presented itself. A young woman, modest but good looking, was standing before a store window gazing with interest at its display of shaving mugs and inkstands. Two yards from the window, a large, stern-looking policeman leaned against a fire hydrant.

It was Soapy's plan to assume the role of the "masher."[15] The elegant and **refined**[16] appearance of his victim and the nearness of the watchful cop encouraged him to believe that he would soon feel the pleasant official clutch upon his arm that would insure his stay at the Island.

Soapy straightened the lady missionary's ready-made tie, dragged his shirtcuffs over his wrists, set his hat at an angle, and walked over towards the woman. He made eyes at her, coughed a bit, smiled, **smirked**,[17] and shamelessly went through the routine

---

[15] masher—man who makes advances (or "passes") at a woman he doesn't know.

[16] **refined**—gracious; well-dressed.

[17] **smirked**—smiled in a familiar or smug way.

of the masher. With half an eye, Soapy saw the policeman watching him carefully. The young woman moved away a few steps and again stared at the shaving mugs. Soapy followed, boldly stepping to her side, raised his hat and said:

"Ah there, Bedelia! Don't you want to come and play in my yard?"

The policeman was still looking. All the **persecuted**[18] young woman would have to do was raise a finger, and Soapy would be practically on the way to his winter home on the Island. Already he imagined he could feel the cozy warmth of the police station. The young woman faced him and, stretching out a hand, caught Soapy's coat sleeve.

"Sure, Mike," she said, joyfully, "if you'll buy me a beer! I'd have spoken to you sooner, but that cop was watching." With the young woman clinging like a vine to his arm, Soapy walked past the policeman overcome with gloom. He seemed doomed to liberty.

At the next corner, he shook off his friend and ran. He stopped in a wealthy district and watched as women in furs and men in heavy overcoats moved gaily in the wintry air. A sudden fear came over Soapy. Had some dreadful magic made him

---

[18] **persecuted**—harassed; annoyed.

immune[19] to arrest? Feeling panicky, Soapy resumed walking. When he next came upon a policeman, he fell into his best "disorderly conduct" routine. He began to yell drunken **gibberish**[20] at the top of his harsh voice. He danced, howled, raved, and otherwise disturbed the peace.

> *He danced, howled, raved, and otherwise disturbed the peace.*

The policeman twirled his club, turned his back, and remarked to a citizen:

"It's one of them Yale[21] lads celebratin' the team's win over Hartford College. They're noisy but harmless. We've been told to let them be."

Soapy couldn't believe it. Still no arrest. In his mind, the Island was starting to seem like an unreachable Arcadia.[22] Disgusted, he buttoned his thin coat against the chilling wind.

In a cigar store he saw a well-dressed man lighting a cigar. Soapy noticed that the man had put his silk umbrella by the door upon entering. Soapy stepped inside, grabbed the umbrella, and walked off with it slowly. The man with the cigar followed hastily.

---

[19] **immune**—protected against.

[20] **gibberish**—nonsense.

[21] Yale—university in New Haven, Connecticut.

[22] Arcadia—place in ancient Greece where everyone supposedly lived in simplicity and perfect happiness.

"My umbrella," he said, sternly.

"Oh, is it?" sneered Soapy in a nasty way. "Well, why don't you call a policeman? I took your umbrella! Why don't you call a cop? There's one there, on that corner."

The umbrella owner slowed his steps. Soapy did likewise, with a feeling that luck would once again run against him. The policeman looked at the two curiously.

"Of course—" said the umbrella man, "that is—well, you know how these mistakes occur and I—and if it's your umbrella, I hope you'll excuse me—I picked it up this morning in a restaurant. If you recognize it as yours, why—I hope you'll—"

"Of course it's mine," said Soapy in a nasty way.

The ex-umbrella man left. The policeman turned away and hurried to assist a tall blonde who was trying to cross the street in front of a street car that was still blocks away.

Soapy continued walking eastward through a street that was being damaged by improvements. He hurled the umbrella into a building site and muttered against the men who wear helmets and carry clubs. Because he wanted to fall into the police's hands, they seemed to regard him as a king who could do no wrong.

At length Soapy reached one of the avenues to the east where it was much quieter. He set his face toward Madison Square, for the **homing instinct**[23] survives even when the home is a park bench.

But on an unusually quiet corner, Soapy came to a standstill. Here was an old church, **quaint**[24] and rambling. Through one violet-stained window, a soft light glowed invitingly. Soapy could hear the sweet music of the organist, who was no doubt practicing for this coming Sunday's services. The music was so lovely that Soapy stood **transfixed**[25] by the iron fence.

T he moon was above, bright and lovely. There were few vehicles and even fewer people on the street. Sparrows twittered sleepily on the roof of the church. With a smile on his face, Soapy listened to the beautiful music. He knew the tune well, for he had heard it often, back when his life had held such things as mothers and roses and dreams and friends and **immaculate**[26] thoughts and collars.

---

[23] **homing instinct**—urge to return home.

[24] **quaint**—attractive in an old-fashioned way.

[25] **transfixed**—made motionless by awe.

[26] **immaculate**—totally clean and pure.

Because he was in such an open state of mind, and because he was standing so close to this old church, an unexpected and wonderful change suddenly took place in Soapy's soul. He thought with quick horror about the pit into which he had tumbled. He thought about the **degraded**[27] days, the unworthy desires, dead hopes, and **base**[28] motives that made up his life.

> *Because he was in such an open state of mind, and because he was standing so close to this old church, an unexpected and wonderful change suddenly took place in Soapy's soul.*

In a moment, his heart responded thrillingly to this new mood. He decided on the spot that he would make a fresh start. He would pull himself out of the dirt. He would make a man of himself again. He would fight against the evil that had taken possession of him. There was time; he was still young. He would think again about his old dreams and pursue them once more. Those solemn but sweet organ notes had set up a **revolution**[29] in him. Tomorrow he

---

[27] **degraded**—lowered in dignity; dishonorable.

[28] **base**—without decency or morals.

[29] **revolution**—major change.

would go into the roaring downtown district and find work. A fur importer had once offered him a job as a driver. He would find the man tomorrow and ask for the position. He would be somebody in the world. He would—

Soapy felt a hand on his arm. He looked quickly around into the broad face of a policeman.

"What are you doin' here?" asked the officer.

"Nothin'," said Soapy.

"Then come along," said the policeman.

"Three months on the Island, for the crime of loitering,"[30] said the judge in the Police Court the next morning.

THE END

---

[30] loitering—standing about with no purpose.

A Madison Square Arabian Night

After he receives a disturbing letter, Carson Chalmers feels the need for something new and different. To make his evening more interesting, Chalmers invites a man from the street to dinner. Because of this kind act, he makes a great discovery.

To Carson Chalmers, in his apartment near the square, Phillips, the butler, brought the evening mail. Besides the routine letters and bills, there were two items with the same foreign postmark.

One of the incoming packages contained a photograph of a woman. The other contained an endless letter, which Chalmers took a long time to read. The letter was from another woman, and it contained a series of poisonous insults, sweetly dipped in honey, and all sorts of other rumors and gossip about the woman in the photograph.

Chalmers tore this letter into a thousand bits and began to wear out his expensive rug by walking back and forth upon it like a wild animal in a cage. This way a caged man acts when he is full of doubt.

By and by, Chalmers was able to shove his anxiety to the back of his mind. The rug was not a magic one. He could only walk sixteen feet on it. He couldn't help someone three thousand miles away.

At this moment, Phillips the butler appeared again, reminding Chalmers once again of a magic **genie**[1] who always knew the exact moment to appear and disappear.

"Will you have dinner here, sir, or out?" Phillips asked.

"Here," said Chalmers, "and in half an hour." He listened sadly to the January wind blowing through the empty streets.

"Wait," he said to the disappearing genie. "As I came home across the end of the square, I saw many men standing there in rows. There was one standing

---

[1] **genie**—a magic spirit that grants wishes. The references here and throughout the story are to *The Arabian Nights*. It is a collection of magical tales of Aladdin, Ali Baba, and Sinbad the Sailor that have fascinated children and adults alike for hundreds of years.

on a box and talking. Why do those men stand in rows, and why are they there?"

"They are homeless men, sir," said Phillips. "The man standing on the box tries to get lodging for them for the night. People come around to listen and give him money. Then he sends as many as the money will pay for to some lodging house. That is why they stand in rows. They get sent to bed in order as they come."

> *On that night, he felt he would have to do something different, something surprising.*

"By the time dinner is served," said Chalmers, "have one of those men here. He will dine with me."

"W-w-which—," began Phillips, stammering for the first time since he'd worked for Chalmers. "Choose one at random," said Chalmers. "You might see that he is reasonably **sober**[2]—and a certain amount of cleanliness will not be held against him. That is all."

It was an unusual thing for Carson Chalmers to act like a Caliph.[3] But on that night, he felt he would have to do something different, something surprising,

---

[2] **sober**—not drunk.

[3] Caliph—religious and civil head of a Muslim state. O. Henry uses the word to give an Arabian flavor to his story.

to help himself out of his sad state of mind. He needed to do something **wanton**[4] and new, something fancy and Arabian, to make him feel better.

A half hour later, the waiters from the restaurant below had brought up a tasty dinner. The dining table, set for two, glowed cheerily with the flames of the pink-shaded candles. And then Phillips brought in a shivering guest who had been pulled from the line of poor men on the square.

I t is a common thing to call such men "wrecks," for they are indeed wrecked in their appearance. Even so, this man had a fire in his eyes that Chalmers noticed right away. His face and hands had been recently washed, an act the genie Phillips had demanded. In the candlelight he stood, a **flaw**[5] in the dignity of the apartment. His face was a sickly white, covered almost to the eyes with a beard the shade of a red Irish setter's coat.[6] Phillips's comb had failed to control the matted pale brown hair that had spent so many long months under a hat. His eyes were full of the kind of hopeless, tricky **defiance**[7] that you might see in a dog's eyes when

---

[4] **wanton**—risky.

[5] **flaw**—defect that stops something from being perfect.

[6] Irish setter's coat—the reddish hair of a large breed of dog.

[7] **defiance**—daring manner.

he is cornered. His shabby coat was buttoned high, but a quarter inch of white collar showed above it. His manner was strangely free from embarrassment when Chalmers rose from his chair across the round dining table.

"If you will allow it," said the host, "I would be glad to have you join me for dinner."

"My name is Plumer," said the guest from the street, in harsh and aggressive tones. "If you're like me, you like to know the name of the party you're dining with."

"I was going on to say," continued Chalmers somewhat hastily, "that mine is Chalmers. Will you sit here, please?"

Plumer, of the ruffled plumes,[8] bent his knees for Phillips to slide the chair beneath him. He had an air of having sat at fine dining tables before. Phillips set out the appetizers and olives.

"Good!" barked Plumer. "We're going to have dinner in courses,[9] correct? All right, my cheerful ruler of Baghdad.[10] I'm your Scheherezade[11] all the

---

[8] ruffled plumes—like an upset bird; offended.

[9] dinner in courses—food served in stages. For example, the salad is served first, then the fish, then the meat, and so on.

[10] Baghdad—a city in Iraq, another reference to legendary Arabia.

[11] Scheherezade—the main storyteller of The Arabian Nights.

way to the toothpicks. You're the first Caliph with a genuine Oriental flavor I've come across since frost. What luck! And I was forty-third in line. I had just finished counting the men ahead of me when your messenger arrived to invite me to your feast. I had about as much chance of getting a bed tonight as I have of being the next president.

You're the first Caliph with a genuine Oriental flavor I've come across since frost.

"So! How will you have the sad story of my life? Would you like a chapter with each course of the meal or the whole edition with the cigars and coffee?"

"This situation does not seem to be a new one to you," said Chalmers with a smile.

"By heavens, no!" answered the guest. "I've been held up for my story with a loaded meal pointed at my head twenty times. Try to catch anybody in New York giving you something for nothing!

"New Yorkers spell curiosity and charity with the same set of alphabet blocks. Lots of 'em will give you a dime and a plate of stew, and a few of 'em will offer a sirloin steak. But every one of 'em will stand over you till they screw your autobiography out of you with footnotes, **appendix**,[12] and unpublished bits and pieces.

"Oh, I know what to do when I see food coming toward me in little old Baghdad-on-the-Subway.[13] I pound the pavement three times with my forehead and get ready to tell stories for my supper. After all, I am related to the late Tommy Tucker,[14] who was forced to sing himself hoarse for oatmeal and soup.

"I do not ask your story," said Chalmers. "I tell you frankly that it was a sudden **whim**[15] that prompted me to send for some stranger to dine with me. I assure you, you will not suffer through any curiosity of mine."

"Oh, fudge!" exclaimed the guest, enthusiastically tackling his soup, "I don't mind it a bit. I'm a regular Oriental magazine with a red cover when you Caliphs walk about. In fact, we fellows in the bed line have a sort of union rate for things of this kind. Somebody's always stopping and asking what brought us down so low in the world. For a sandwich and a glass of beer I tell 'em that drink did it. For corned beef and cabbage and a cup of coffee, I give 'em the hard hearted-landlord-six-

---

[12] **appendix**—information at the end of a book.

[13] Baghdad-on-the-Subway—O. Henry's favorite name for New York City.

[14] Tommy Tucker—a reference to the nursery rhyme character, little Tommy Tucker, who sang for his supper.

[15] **whim**—decision that can't be understood.

months-in-the-hospital-lost-job story. A sirloin steak and a quarter for a bed gets the Wall Street[16] tragedy of the swept-away fortune and the slow descent into poverty.

"But this is the first meal of this kind that I've ever stumbled upon, so I haven't got a story to fit it. I'll tell you what, Mr. Chalmers. I'm going to tell you the truth as payback for this meal, if you'll listen to it. The truth will be harder for you to believe than the made-up stories."

"I'm going to tell you the truth as payback for this meal, if you'll listen to it. The truth will be harder for you to believe than the made-up stories."

An hour later, the Arabian guest sat back with a sigh of satisfaction. Then Phillips brought the coffee and cigars and cleared the table.

"Did you ever hear of Sherrard Plumer?" the guest asked, with a strange smile.

"I remember the name," said Chalmers. "He was a painter, I think, who was well-regarded a few years ago."

"Five years," said the guest. "Then I went down like a chunk of lead. I'm Sherrard Plumer! I sold the

---

[16] Wall Street—New York City street known for its financial dealings.

last portrait I painted for $2,000. After that, I couldn't have found a sitter for a free picture."

"What was the trouble?" Chalmers could not resist asking.

"Well, it's a funny thing," answered Plumer grimly. "I never quite understood it myself. For a while I swam like a cork.[17] I broke into the fancy crowd and got painting jobs right and left. The newspapers called me a fashionable painter. Then the funny things began to happen. Whenever I finished a picture, people would come and see it and whisper and look strangely at each other.

"I soon found out what the trouble was. I had a **knack**[18] for bringing out in the face of a portrait the hidden character of the person I was painting. I don't know how I did it—I painted what I saw. But I know that it did me in. Some of the people I painted were so angry that they refused to pay for their pictures.

"For example, I painted the portrait of a very beautiful and popular society woman. When it was finished, her husband looked at it with a strange expression on his face, and the next week he filed for divorce. Another time, a wealthy banker asked

---

[17] swam like a cork—did very well.
[18] **knack**—talent.

to have his picture painted. When I put his portrait on display in my studio, an acquaintance of his came in to look at it. 'Bless me,' says he, 'does he really look like that?' I told him the picture looked just like the man. 'I never noticed that expression in his eyes before,' said he. 'I think I'll drop downtown and change my bank account.' He did go down to the bank, but the account was gone and so was Mr. Banker.

"It wasn't long before they put me out of business. People don't want their secret meanness shown up in a picture. In real life, they can smile and twist their own faces and **deceive**[19] you, but the picture can't. I couldn't get an order for another picture, and I had to give up.

"I worked as a newspaper artist for a while and then for a printer, but my work for them got me into the same trouble. If I drew from a photograph, my drawing showed up things and expressions that you couldn't find in the photo—but I guess they were in the original, all right. The customers complained, especially the women, and I never could hold a job long. So I began to rest my weary head upon the breast of Old Booze[20] for comfort. And pretty soon I

---

[19] **deceive**—lie to.

[20] Old Booze—alcoholic drink.

was in the free-bed line and making up stories for handouts among the food **bazaars**.[21]

"Does the truth make you tired, O Caliph? I can turn on the Wall Street disaster story if you prefer. But that requires a tear in my eye, and I'm afraid I can't hustle one up after that good dinner."

"No, no," said Chalmers, **earnestly**.[22] "You interest me very much. Did all of your portraits reveal some ugly trait, or were there some pictures that did not suffer from your knack?"

"Some? Yes, there were some," said Plumer. "Children generally, a good many women, and enough of men. All people aren't bad, you know. When the people were all right, the pictures were all right. As I said, I don't explain it, but I'm telling you facts."

On Chalmers's desk lay the photograph that he had received that day in the foreign mail. Ten minutes later he had Plumer at work making a sketch from it in **pastels**.[23] At the end of an hour, the artist rose and stretched wearily.

"It's done," he yawned. "You'll excuse me for taking so long. I got interested in the job. Whoa, but I'm tired! No bed last night, you know. Guess

---

[21] **bazaars**—marketplaces, particularly in the Middle East.

[22] **earnestly**—seriously.

[23] **pastels**—chalk-like crayons.

I'll have to say good night now, O Commander of the Faithful!"

Chalmers walked to the door with the man and slipped some bills into his hand.

"Oh! I'll take your money," said Plumer, "and thank you for it, and for the very good dinner. I shall sleep on feathers tonight and dream of Baghdad. I hope it won't turn out to be a dream in the morning. Farewell, most excellent Caliph!"

Again Chalmers paced restlessly upon his rug, trying to stay as far away as he could from the pastel sketch. Twice, three times, he tried to approach it, but failed. He could see the **dun**[24] and gold and brown of the colors, but there was a wall around it, built by his own fears that kept him at a distance. He sat down and tried to calm himself. Then, he jumped up and rang for Phillips.

"There is a young artist in this building," he said, "a Mr. Reineman. Do you know which is his apartment?"

"He lives on the top floor, sir," said Phillips.

"Go up and ask him to be kind enough to come down here for a moment or two."

---

[24] **dun**—grayish-brown.

Reineman came at once. Chalmers introduced himself.

"Mr. Reineman," said he, "there is a little pastel sketch on that desk. I would be glad if you will give me your opinion of it."

The young artist moved to the table and took up the sketch. Chalmers half turned away, leaning upon the back of his chair.

"What—do—you—think of it?" Chalmers asked, slowly.

"As a drawing," said the artist, "I can't praise it enough. It's the work of a master! It is bold and fine and true. It puzzles me a little; I haven't seen any pastel work nearly this good in years."

"The face, man! The subject—the woman— what do you say about her?" Chalmers asked in a pleading voice.

"The face," said Reineman, "is the face of one of God's own angels. May I ask who—"

"It's my wife!" shouted Chalmers, wheeling and pouncing upon the astonished artist, shaking his hand and pounding his back. "She is traveling in Europe. Take that sketch, boy, and paint the picture of your life from it and leave the price to me."

THE END

Con Men

A Retrieved Reformation

In this story, a slick bank robber falls in love. He decides to turn his life around and become an honest citizen. Will the policeman who is chasing him believe in the thief's change of heart?

A guard came to the prison shoeshop where Jimmy Valentine was busily sewing shoes and took him to the front office. There the warden handed Jimmy his pardon, which had been signed that morning by the governor. Jimmy took it in a tired kind of way. He had served nearly ten months of a four-year sentence. He had expected to stay only about three months, at the longest. When a man has as many friends on the outside as Jimmy Valentine had, it's hardly worth the effort to cut his hair when he is first brought to prison.

"Now, Valentine," said the warden, "you'll go out in the morning. Pull yourself together, and make a man of yourself. You're not a bad fellow at heart. Stop cracking safes, and live straight."

"Me?" said Jimmy, in surprise. "Why, I never cracked a safe in my life."

> *"Me?" said Jimmy, in surprise. "Why, I never cracked a safe in my life."*

"Oh, no," laughed the warden. "Of course not. Let's see, now. Why were you found guilty on that Springfield job? Was it simply a case of a mean old jury that had it in for you? It's always one or the other with you innocent victims."

"Me?" said Jimmy, still playing the innocent. "Why, warden, I never was in Springfield in my life!"

"Take him back, guard," smiled the warden, "and fix him up with a set of clothes that he can go home in. Unlock him at seven in the morning, and let him come to my office. And you, Valentine. Think about my advice."

At 7:15 the next morning, Jimmy stood in the warden's office. He had on the ill-fitting suit and the pair of squeaky shoes that the state gives to every prisoner on his way out.

The clerk handed Valentine a railroad ticket and the five-dollar bill with which the law expected him to **rehabilitate**[1] himself.

The warden gave him a cigar, and shook hands. Then the clerk wrote, "Valentine 9762, Pardoned by Governor" on the books, and Mr. James Valentine walked out into the sunshine.

Ignoring the song of the birds, the waving green trees, and the smell of the flowers, Jimmy headed straight for a restaurant. There he tasted the first sweet joys of liberty in the shape of a broiled chicken, a bottle of white wine, and a cigar that was quite a bit better than the one the warden had given him. From there he walked slowly to the train depot. He tossed a quarter into the hat of a blind man sitting by the door, and then he boarded his train. Three hours later, he got off in a little town near the state line. He went to the restaurant owned by Mike Dolan and shook hands with Mike, who was alone behind the bar.

"Sorry we couldn't get you out sooner, Jimmy, me boy," said Mike. "But we had a few problems in Springfield, and the governor nearly refused to let you out. Feeling all right?"

"Fine," said Jimmy. "Got my key?"

---

[1] **rehabilitate**—retrain; restore to goodness.

He got his key and went upstairs, unlocking the door of a room at the rear. Everything was just as he had left it. Still on the floor was Detective Ben Price's shirt button that had been torn from his shirt when he had come to arrest Jimmy.

Pulling out from the wall a folding bed, Jimmy slid back a panel in the wall and dragged out a dust-covered suitcase. He opened this and gazed fondly at the finest set of burglar's tools in the East. It was a complete set, made of an especially strong steel, the latest designs in drills, braces and bits, jimmies,[2] clamps, and augers,[3] with two or three items invented by Jimmy himself, in which he took pride. Over nine hundred dollars these tools had cost him, and he loved them dearly.

In half an hour, Jimmy went downstairs and through the diner. He was now dressed in tasteful and well-fitting clothes and carried his dusted and cleaned suitcase in his hand.

"Got any plans?" asked Mike Dolan, in a friendly way.

"Me?" said Jimmy, in a puzzled tone. "I don't understand. I'm a salesman for the New York State Short Snap Biscuit Cracker and Worn-Out Wheat Company."

---

[2] jimmies—tools for forcing doors open.
[3] augers—tools used for boring holes.

This statement made Mike so happy that he gave Jimmy a seltzer[4]-and-milk on the spot. Jimmy never touched liquor.

A week after the release of Valentine 9762, there was a neat safe-burglary done in Richmond, Indiana, with no clues left on the scene. The burglar was able to pick up eight hundred dollars there. Two weeks after that, a new and improved burglar-proof safe in Logansport was easily opened to the tune of fifteen hundred dollars. At this point, the police sat up and took notice. Then, an old-fashioned bank safe in Jefferson City was cracked and five thousand dollars was stolen. The losses were now high enough that Detective Ben Price was assigned to the case. By comparing notes, Ben Price noticed that the burglaries were all remarkably similar. He paid a visit to the scenes of the crimes and was heard to remark:

"This is Dandy[5] Jim Valentine's work. He's back in business, I see. Look at that safe lock. It's been yanked out as easy as pulling up a radish in wet weather. He's got the only clamps that can do it. And look how clean those tumblers[6] were punched out! Jimmy never has to drill more than one hole. Yes, I

---

[4] seltzer—carbonated water.

[5] Dandy—name for a man who is a fancy dresser.

[6] tumblers—levers.

guess I want Mr. Valentine. He'll stay in prison the next time, without any pardon from the governor."

Ben Price knew Jimmy's habits. He had learned them while working on the Springfield case. Quick getaways, no helpers, and a taste for good society had helped Mr. Valentine avoid being caught. But, when it was announced that Ben Price was on the trail of the **elusive**[7] burglar, people with burglar-proof safes began to feel safe once again.

Jimmy Valentine looked into her eyes, forgot what he was, and became another man.

One afternoon, Jimmy Valentine and his suitcase jumped off the train in Elmore, a little town in Arkansas. Jimmy, looking like an athletic young senior just home from college, went down the sidewalk toward the hotel.

A young lady crossed the street, passed him at the corner, and entered a door over which was the sign "The Elmore Bank." Jimmy Valentine looked into her eyes, forgot what he was, and became another man. She lowered her eyes and colored slightly. Young men of Jimmy's style and looks were not often found in Elmore.

---

[7] **elusive**—difficult to catch.

Jimmy went up to a boy who was hanging around the steps of the bank and began to ask him questions about the town, feeding him dimes at times. By and by the young lady came out. She pretended not to notice Jimmy, and went her way.

"Isn't that young lady Miss Polly Simpson?" asked Jimmy, pretending to look confused.

"Naw," said the boy. "She's Annabel Adams. Her pa owns this bank. What'd you come to Elmore for? Is that a gold watch-chain? I'm going to get a bulldog. Got any more dimes?"

Jimmy went to the Planters' Hotel, registered as Ralph D. Spencer, and asked for a room. He leaned on the desk and told his newest story to the clerk. He said he had come to Elmore to look for a location to go into business. How was the shoe business, now, in the town? He had thought about going into the shoe business. Was there an opening?

The clerk was impressed by the clothes and manner of Jimmy. He answered that yes, there might be an opening in the shoe business. There wasn't a shoe store in town. He hoped Mr. Spencer would decide to settle in Elmore. He would find it a pleasant town to live in, and the people very friendly.

Mr. Spencer said he thought he might stay in the town a few days and look over the situation.

Mr. Ralph Spencer—the former Mr. Jimmy Valentine—stayed in Elmore and opened a shoe store. Business was good and life was fine.

Socially he was also a success and made many friends. He met Miss Annabel Adams, and became more and more charmed by her.

At the end of a year, the situation of Mr. Ralph Spencer was this: He had won the respect of the community, his shoe store was doing very well, and he and Annabel were engaged to be married in two weeks. Mr. Adams, a typical country banker, approved of Spencer. He was welcomed into the Adams home and treated like one of the family.

One day Jimmy sat down in his room and wrote this letter, which he mailed to the safe address of one of his old friends in St. Louis:

> *Dear Old Pal:*
>
> *I want you to be at Sullivan's place, in Little Rock, next Wednesday night at 9 o'clock. I want you to wind up a few matters for me. And also, I want to give you my kit of tools. I know you'll be glad to get them—you couldn't duplicate the lot for a thousand dollars.*
>
> *Say, Billy, I've quit the old business—a year ago. I've got a nice store. I'm making an honest living, and I'm going to marry the finest girl on*

Earth two weeks from now. It's the only life,
Billy, the straight one. I wouldn't touch a dollar
of another man's money for a million. After I get
married, I'm going to sell my business and go
West, where there won't be so much danger of
having old scores[8] brought up against me.

I tell you, Billy, she's an angel. She believes in
me, and I wouldn't do another crooked thing for
the whole world. Be sure to be at Sullivan's, for I
must see you. I'll bring along the tools with me.

Your old friend,
Jimmy

On the Monday night after Jimmy wrote this letter, Ben Price made a secret trip into Elmore. He lounged about town in his quiet way until he found out what he wanted to know. From the drug store across the street from Spencer's shoe store, he got a good look at Ralph D. Spencer.

"Going to marry the banker's daughter are you, Jimmy?" said Ben to himself, softly. "Well, I don't know about that!"

The next morning Jimmy ate breakfast at the Adams's house. He was going to Little Rock that day to order his wedding suit and buy something nice for Annabel. That would be the first time he

---

[8] scores—crimes.

had left town since he came to Elmore. It had been more than a year now since those last professional "jobs," and he thought he could safely travel about.

After breakfast, the whole family set out together—Mr. Adams, Annabel, Jimmy, and Annabel's married sister with her two little girls, aged five and nine. They walked to the hotel where Jimmy was still living, and he ran up to his room and got his suitcase. Then they went on to the bank. At the bank stood Jimmy's horse and buggy and Dolph Gibson, who was going to drive him over to the railroad station.

The group went inside past the high, carved oak railings and into the banking-room—Jimmy included, for Mr. Adams's future son-in-law was welcome anywhere. The clerks were pleased to be greeted by the good-looking, pleasant young man who was going to marry Miss Annabel. Jimmy set his suitcase down. Annabel, who was in a playful mood, put on Jimmy's hat and picked up the suitcase. "Wouldn't I make a nice salesman?" said Annabel. "My! Ralph, how heavy this suitcase is. It feels like it is full of gold bricks."

"I've got a bunch of metal shoehorns[9] in there," said Jimmy, coolly. "I'm going to return them while

---

[9] shoehorns—devices that help people put their shoes on.

I'm in Little Rock, to save myself the charge of mailing them. I'm becoming awfully careful with my money."

The Elmore Bank had just put in a new safe and vault. Mr. Adams was very proud of it and insisted on giving everyone a quick look. The vault was a small one, but it had a new door. It fastened with three solid steel bolts that could be locked with a single handle, and it had a time lock. Mr. Adams proudly explained its workings to Mr. Spencer, who showed a polite but not too intelligent interest. The two children, May and Agatha, were delighted by the shining metal and funny clock and knobs.

Suddenly there was a scream or two from the women and general confusion.

While they were busy looking at the safe, Ben Price wandered into the bank and leaned on his elbow, looking casually inside between the railings. He told the teller that he didn't want anything, he was just waiting for a man he knew.

Suddenly there was a scream or two from the women and general confusion. It turned out that May, the nine-year-old girl, had playfully shut Agatha in the vault. She had turned the handle that locked the bolts and twirled the knob of the combination lock as she had seen Mr. Adams do.

The old banker sprang to the handle and tugged at it for a moment. "The door can't be opened," he groaned. "The clock hasn't been wound and the combination has not been set!"

Agatha's mother screamed again, in her highest voice.

"Hush!" said Mr. Adams, raising his trembling hand. "All be quiet for a moment. Agatha!" he called as loudly as he could.

"Listen to me." During the following silence they could just hear the faint sound of the child's terrified shrieking in the dark vault.

"My precious darling!" wailed the mother. "She will die of fright! Open the door! Oh, break it open! Can't you men do something?"

"There isn't a man nearer than Little Rock who can open that door," said Mr. Adams, in a shaky voice. "Spencer, what shall we do? That child—she can't stand it long in there. There isn't enough air, and, besides, she'll die from fright."

Agatha's mother, frantic now, beat the door of the vault with her hands. Somebody wildly suggested dynamite.[10] Annabel turned to Jimmy, her large eyes full of fear and worry, but not yet despairing. Surely her darling Ralph could find a way to get the child out!

---

[10] dynamite—an explosive.

"Can't you do something, Ralph? Try, won't you?"

He looked at her with a strange, soft smile on his lips and in his intelligent eyes.

"Annabel," he said, "give me that rose you are wearing, will you?"

Hardly believing that she heard him correctly, she unpinned the rose from the front of her dress, and placed it in his hand. Jimmy stuffed it into his vest pocket, threw off his coat, and pulled up his sleeves. With that act, Ralph D. Spencer passed away and Jimmy Valentine took his place.

"Get away from the door, all of you," he commanded, shortly. He set his suitcase on the table, and opened it out flat. From that time on, he ignored everyone else around him. He laid out the shining, strange tools swiftly and in order, whistling softly to himself as he always did when at work. Silently the others watched him as if they were under a magic spell.

In a minute, Jimmy's favorite drill was biting smoothly into the steel door. In ten minutes— breaking his own burglary record—he threw back the bolts and opened the door.

Agatha, close to fainting, but safe, was gathered into her mother's arms.

Jimmy Valentine put on his coat and walked outside the railings toward the front door. As he went towards the front door, he thought he heard a far-away voice that he once knew call "Ralph!" But he never hesitated.

At the door a big man stood somewhat in his way.

"Hello, Ben!" said Jimmy, still with his strange smile. "Found me at last, haven't you? Well, let's go. I don't know that it makes much difference, now."

And then Detective Price acted rather strangely.

"Guess you're mistaken, Mr. Spencer," he said. "Don't believe I recognize you at all. Your buggy's waiting for you, ain't it?"

And Ben Price turned and strolled down the street.

THE END

After Twenty Years

Two young men make a promise to themselves and each other. No matter where they are or what they are doing, they'll meet at a New York City restaurant after twenty years have gone by.

The policeman on the beat[1] moved up the avenue **impressively**.[2] The impressiveness was his habit, not for show, because there were few people on the street. It was barely 10 o'clock at night, but chilly gusts of wind and the smell of rain had nearly cleared the street.

The officer checked doors as he went, twirling his club with many complicated and skillful movements.

---

[1] beat—territory or area that a policeman covers.

[2] **impressively**—in a way that makes people respect him.

With his strong form and slight **swagger**,[3] the officer looked like a fine guardian of the peace.

Very few places stayed open this late at night. Now and then you might see the lights of a cigar store or of an all-night diner, but the majority of the doors belonged to businesses that had long since closed for the night.

About midway down the block, the policeman suddenly slowed his walk. In the doorway of a darkened hardware store a man leaned, with an unlighted cigar in his mouth.

As the policeman walked up to him, the man spoke up quickly. "It's all right, officer," he said, calmly, "I'm just waiting for a friend. It's an appointment made twenty years ago. Sounds a little funny to you, doesn't it? Well, I'll explain if you'd like to make certain it's all straight. About that long ago, there used to be a restaurant where this store stands—'Big Joe' Brady's restaurant."

"It was here until five years ago," said the policeman. "Then it was torn down."

The man in the doorway struck a match and lit his cigar. The light showed a pale, square-jawed face with **keen**[4] eyes and a little white scar near his right eyebrow. The pin on his scarf had a large,

---

[3] **swagger**—self-confident walk.

[4] **keen**—sharp, strong.

oddly set diamond. "Twenty years ago tonight," said the man, "I dined here at 'Big Joe' Brady's with Jimmy Wells, my best chum and the finest man in the world. He and I were raised here in New York, just like two brothers, together. I was eighteen and Jimmy was twenty. The next morning, I was to start for the West to make my fortune. You couldn't have dragged Jimmy out of New York. He thought it was the only place on Earth. Well, we agreed that night that we would meet here again exactly twenty years from that date and time, no matter what our conditions might be or from what distance we might have to come. We figured that in twenty years each of us ought to have our **destiny**[5] worked out and our fortunes made, whatever they were going to be."

"It sounds pretty interesting," said the policeman. "Rather a long time between meetings, though, it seems to me. Haven't you heard from your friend since you left?"

"Well, yes, for a time we wrote letters," said the man. "But after a year or two we lost track of each other. You see, the West is a pretty big place, and I kept hustling back and forth quite a bit. But I know

---

[5] **destiny**—future life.

Jimmy will meet me here if he's alive, for he always was the truest, most trustworthy man in the world. He'll never forget. I came a thousand miles to stand in this door tonight, and it's worth it if my old partner turns up.

The waiting man pulled out a handsome watch, the lids of it set with small diamonds. "Three minutes to ten," he announced. "It was exactly ten o'clock when we parted here at the restaurant door."

"You did pretty well for yourself out West, didn't you?" asked the policeman.

"You bet! I hope Jimmy has done half as well. He was a kind of plodder,[6] though, even though he was a good fellow. I've had to compete with some of the sharpest wits when I was putting together my pile of money. A man gets too comfortable in New York. It takes the West to put a sharp edge on him."

The policeman twirled his club, took a step or two, and said, "I'll be on my way. Hope your friend comes around all right. Are you going to leave at 10 o'clock sharp if he doesn't show up?"

"I should say not!" said the other. "I'll give him half an hour at least. If Jimmy is alive on Earth, he'll be here by that time. So long, officer."

"Good-night, sir," said the policeman, passing on along his beat, trying doors as he went.

---

[6] plodder—person who is slow and steady.

There was now a fine, cold drizzle falling, and the wind had risen to a steady blow. The few people on the street hurried quickly along with coat collars turned up high and pocketed hands. And in the door of the hardware store, the man who had come a thousand miles to meet up with a friend of his youth smoked his cigar and waited.

About twenty minutes he waited, and then a tall man in a long overcoat, with collar turned up to his ears, hurried across from the opposite side of the street. He went directly to the waiting man.

"Is that you, Bob?" he asked, doubtfully.

"Is that you, Jimmy Wells?" cried the man in the door.

"Bless my heart!" exclaimed the new arrival, grasping both the other's hands with his own. "It's Bob, sure as can be. I was certain I'd find you here if you were still in existence. Well, well, well! Twenty years is a long time. The old restaurant's gone, Bob; I wish it had lasted, so we could have had another dinner there. How has the West treated you, old man?"

"Great. It has given me everything I asked it for. You've changed lots, Jimmy. I picture you two or three inches shorter."

"Oh, I grew a bit after I was twenty."

"Doing well in New York, Jimmy?"

"Fairly well. I have a job with the city. Come on, Bob; we'll go around to a place I know of and have a good long talk about old times."

The two men started up the street, arm in arm. The man from the West, his pride enlarged by success, was beginning to outline the history of his career. The other, still huddled in his overcoat, listened with interest.

At the corner stood a drug store, brilliant with electric lights. When they came into the light, each of them turned at the same time to gaze upon the other's face.

The man from the West stopped suddenly and released his arm. "You're not Jimmy Wells," he snapped. Twenty years is a long time, but not long enough to change a man's nose from a Roman to a pug."[7]

"Twenty years sometimes changes a good man into a bad one," said the tall man. "You've been under arrest for ten minutes, 'Silky' Bob. The police in Chicago thought you might be in New York about now, so they sent us your photo and asked us to have a chat with you. Going quietly, are you?

---

[7] a Roman to a pug—a Roman nose is long and has a wide upper part; a pug nose is short and flat.

That's very wise. Now, before we go to the police station, here's a note I was asked to hand to you. You may read it here at the window. It's from Patrolman Wells."

The man from the West unfolded the little piece of paper handed him. His hand was steady when he began to read, but it shook a little by the time he had finished. The note was rather short:

> Bob,
>
> I was at the appointed place on time. When you lit the match for your cigar, I saw the face of the man wanted in Chicago. Somehow I couldn't arrest you myself, so I went around and got a plainclothes officer to do the job.
>
> —Jimmy

THE END

The Ransom of Red Chief

In this very funny story, two thugs decide to kidnap a boy so that they can collect some quick ransom money. Unfortunately, they choose the wrong boy.

It looked like a good thing, but wait till I tell you. We were down South, in Alabama—Bill Driscoll and myself—when this kidnapping idea struck us. We had the idea, as Bill said afterwards, "during a moment of temporary mental apparition,"[1] but we didn't find that out till later.

---

[1] mental apparition—Bill meant to say "mental aberration," or craziness. An apparition is a sudden or unusual appearance, like a ghost. An aberration is a change from what is normal. O. Henry is playing with words.

There was a town down there, as flat as a pancake and called Summit,[2] of course. In Summit lived a group of people as harmless and self-satisfied as any group that ever gathered around a Maypole.[3]

_____

A kidnapping project ought to do better there than in a big city. There, newspapers tend to send reporters out to stir up information.

_____

Bill and me had together about six hundred dollars, and we needed just two thousand dollars more to pull off a phony land deal in Western Illinois. We talked it over on the front steps of the hotel. Families, says we, are strong in rural communities. Privacy is also strong. Therefore, and for other reasons, a kidnapping project ought to do better there than in a big city. There, newspapers tend to send reporters out to stir up information and talk about such things. We knew that Summit couldn't come after us with anything stronger than one police officer and, maybe, a lazy bloodhound or two. So, it looked good.

We selected for our victim the only child of an important citizen named Ebenezer Dorset. The father was respectable and well known. He was a

_____

[2] A summit is a high piece of land. This is another joke.
[3] Maypole—a tall flower-wreathed pole used for May Day sports and dances.

banker with a love of collection-plate passing at church and **foreclosing**.[4] His kid was a boy of ten, with a load of freckles and red hair. Bill and me figured that Ebenezer would hand over a **ransom**[5] of two thousand dollars to a cent. But wait till I tell you.

About two miles from Summit was a little mountain, covered with dense cedar brush. At the rear of this mountain was a cave. There we stored some provisions—food, water, blankets, and so on.

One evening after sundown, we drove in a buggy past old Dorset's house. The kid was in the street, throwing rocks at a kitten on the opposite fence.

"Hey, little boy!" says Bill, "would you like to have a bag of candy and a nice ride?"

The boy catches Bill neatly in the eye with a piece of brick.

"That will cost the old man an extra five hundred dollars," says Bill, climbing over the seat.

That boy put up a fight like a welter-weight[6] brown bear, but at last we got him down into the bottom of the buggy and drove away. We took him up to the cave, and I tied up the horse to a nearby tree. After dark I drove the buggy to the little

---

[4] **foreclosing**—turning a person out of his or her house because of unpaid bills. Usually it's a bank that forecloses on a property.

[5] **ransom**—payment made in order to release a person who has been kidnapped.

[6] welter-weight—in boxing, weighing more than 135 pounds and less than 147 pounds.

village, three miles away, where we'd hired it, and walked back to the mountain.

When I got to our hideout, Bill was putting Band-aids on the scratches and bruises on his face. There was a fire burning behind the big rock at the entrance of the cave, and the boy was watching a pot of boiling coffee, with two buzzard tailfeathers stuck in his red hair. He points a stick at me when I come up, and says:

"Ha! ugly paleface, do you dare to enter the camp of Red Chief, the terror of the Plains?"

"He's all right now," says Bill, rolling up his pants and examining some bruises on his shins. "We're playing Indian. I'm Old Hank, the trapper,[7] Red Chief's prisoner, and I'm to be murdered at daybreak. By Golly, that kid can kick hard!"

Yes, sir, that boy seemed to be having the time of his life. The fun of camping out in a cave had made him forget that he was a prisoner himself. He decided to call me Snake-eye, the spy, and said that, when his Indian braves returned from the warpath, I was to be broiled at the stake[8] at the rising of the sun.

---

[7] trapper—someone who catches animals in order to sell their skins.

[8] broiled at the stake—tied to a piece of wood with a fire beneath; burned at the stake.

Then we had supper; and he filled his mouth full of bacon and bread and gravy, and began to talk. He made a during-dinner speech something like this:

"I like this fine. I never camped out before; but I had a pet 'possum once, and I was nine last birthday. I hate to go to school. Rats ate up sixteen of Jimmy Talbot's aunt's speckled hen's eggs. Are there any real Indians in these woods? I want some more gravy. Does the trees moving make the wind blow? We had five puppies. What makes your nose so red, Hank? My father has lots of money. Are the stars hot? I whipped Ed Walker twice, Saturday. I don't like girls. You can't catch toads unless with a string. Do oxen[9] make any noise? Why are oranges round? Have you got beds to sleep on in this cave? Amos Murray has got six toes. A parrot can talk, but a monkey or a fish can't. How many does it take to make twelve?"

Every few minutes he would remember that he was a warrior, so he would pick up his stick rifle and tiptoe to the mouth of the cave to look for the scouts of the hated paleface. Now and then he would let out a war-whoop that made Old Hank the Trapper shiver. That boy had Bill scared to death from the start.

---

[9] oxen—the plural of *ox*, a type of animal used on a farm.

"Red Chief," says I to the kid, "would you like to go home?"

"Aw, what for?" says he. "I don't have any fun at home. I hate to go to school. I like to camp out. You won't take me back home again, Snake-eye, will you?"

"Not right away," says I. "We'll stay here in the cave a while."

"All right!" says he. "That'll be fine. I never had such fun in all my life."

We went to bed about eleven o'clock. We spread down some wide blankets and quilts and put Red Chief between us. We weren't afraid he'd run away. He kept us awake for three hours, jumping up and reaching for his rifle and screeching: "Hist! partner!" in mine and Bill's ears whenever he heard the crackle of a twig or the rustle of a leaf. At last, I fell into a troubled sleep and dreamed that I had been kidnapped and chained to a tree by an angry pirate with red hair.

Just at daybreak, I was awakened by a series of awful screams from Bill. They weren't yells, or howls, or shouts, or whoops, or yelps, which is what you'd expect from a grown man. Instead, they were terrifying, **humiliating**[10] screams of pure terror.

---

[10] **humiliating**—shaming.

It's an awful thing to hear a strong, desperate, fat man screaming in a cave at daybreak.

I jumped up to see what the matter was. Red Chief was sitting on Bill's chest, with one hand holding fast to Bill's hair. In his other hand he had a sharp knife we used for slicing bacon; and he was busily and realistically trying to cut off Bill's scalp, which he had promised to do the night before.

I got the knife away from the kid and made him lie down again. But, from that moment, Bill's spirit was broken.[11] He laid down on his side of the bed, but he never closed an eye in sleep again as long as that boy was with us. I dozed off for a while, but along toward sunup I remembered that Red Chief had said I was to be burned at the stake at the rising of the sun. I wasn't nervous or afraid; but I sat up and lit my pipe and leaned against a rock.

"What're you getting up so soon for, Sam?" asked Bill.

"Me?" says I. "Oh, I got a kind of a pain in my shoulder. I thought sitting up would rest it."

"You're a liar!" says Bill. "You're afraid. You're to be burned at sunrise, and you're afraid he'll do it. And he would, too, if he could find a match. Ain't

---

[11] broken—totally defeated; crushed.

it awful, Sam? Do you think anybody will pay out money to get a little brat like that back home?"

"Sure," said I. "A rowdy kid like that is just the kind that parents love. Now, you and Red Chief get up and cook breakfast, while I go up on the top of this mountain and look around."

I went up on the peak of the little mountain and looked down toward the little village. I fully expected to see the sturdy men and women of the village armed with scythes and pitchforks[12] beating the countryside for the **dastardly**[13] kidnappers. But what I saw was a peaceful landscape dotted with one man and his mule ploughing his fields. Nobody was dragging the creek;[14] no messengers dashed here and there, bringing information to the terrified parents. There was a sleepy peacefulness to the town. "Perhaps," I said to myself, "it has not yet been discovered that the wolves have kidnapped the tiny lamb. Heaven help the wolves!" says I, and I went down the mountain to breakfast.

When I got to the cave, I found Bill backed up against the side of it, breathing hard. The boy was

---

[12] scythes and pitchforks—farm tools used for mowing grass and stacking hay.

[13] **dastardly**—evil; no good.

[14] dragging the creek—looking for a dead body in the water.

at that moment threatening to smash him with a rock half as big as a coconut.

"He put a red-hot boiled potato down my back," explained Bill, "and then mashed it with his foot, and I boxed[15] his ears. Have you got a gun on you, Sam?"

I took the rock away from the boy and kind of patched up the argument. "I'll fix you," says the kid to Bill. "No man ever struck the Red Chief without paying for it! You'd better watch out!"

_____

"No man ever struck the Red Chief without paying for it! You'd better watch out!"

_____

After breakfast the kid takes a piece of leather with strings wrapped around it out of his pocket and goes outside the cave unwinding it.

"What's he up to now?" says Bill, anxiously. "You don't think he'll run away, do you, Sam?"

"No fear of it," says I. "He don't seem to miss his home too much. But we've got to fix up some plan about the ransom. There don't seem to be much excitement in Summit about the kidnapping. Maybe they haven't realized yet that he's gone. His folks may think he's spending the night with Aunt Jane or one of the neighbors. Anyhow, he'll be missed today. Tonight we must get a message to his

---

[15] boxed—smacked.

father demanding the two thousand dollars for his return."

Just then we heard a kind of warwhoop, such as David might have let out when he knocked out the giant Goliath.[16] It was a slingshot that Red Chief had pulled out of his pocket, and he was whirling it around his head.

I dodged, and heard a heavy thud and a kind of a sigh from Bill, like a horse gives out when you take his saddle off. A rock the size of an egg had caught Bill just behind his left ear. He fell in the fire across the frying pan of hot water for washing the dishes. I dragged him out and poured cold water on his head for half an hour.

By and by, Bill sits up and feels behind his ear and says: "Sam, do you know who my favorite Biblical character is?"

"Take it easy," says I. "You'll come to your senses presently."

"King Herod,"[17] says he. "You won't go away and leave me here alone, will you, Sam?"

---

[16] Goliath—in the Bible, Goliath was a giant killed by David, a boy with a slingshot, a strip of leather with a string fastened to either end and used for throwing stones.

[17] King Herod—King of Judea. According to the Bible, when he learned that Jesus was born, Herod ordered the death of all boys under the age of two in Bethlehem.

I went out and caught that boy and shook him until his freckles rattled.

"If you don't behave," says I, "I'll take you straight home. Now, are you going to be good, or not?"

"I was only having fun," says he **sullenly**.[18] "I didn't mean to hurt Old Hank. But what did he hit me for? I'll behave, Snake-eye, if you won't send me home, and if you'll let me play the Black Scout today."

"I don't know the game," I said. "That's for you and Mr. Bill to decide. He's your playmate for the day. I'm going away for a while, on business. Now, you come in and make friends with him and say you are sorry for hurting him, or home you go, at once."

I made him and Bill shake hands, and then I took Bill aside and told him I was going to Poplar Cove, a little village three miles from the cave, so that I could find out what people were saying about the Summit kidnapping. Also, I thought it would be best to send a letter to old man Dorset that day, demanding the ransom and telling him how it should be paid.

"You know, Sam," says Bill, "I've stood by you in earthquakes, fire, and flood—in poker games,

---

[18] **sullenly**—in a bad-tempered way.

police raids, train robberies, and tornadoes. I never lost my nerve yet till we kidnapped that two-legged skyrocket of a kid. He's got me going. You won't leave me long with him, will you, Sam?"

"I'll be back sometime this afternoon," says I. "You must keep the boy amused and quiet till I return. And now we'll write the letter to old Dorset."

Bill and I got paper and pencil and worked on the letter. Meanwhile, Red Chief, with a blanket wrapped around him, **strutted**[19] up and down, guarding the mouth of the cave. Bill begged me tearfully to make the ransom fifteen hundred dollars instead of two thousand. "Listen, Sam," he said, "we're dealing with humans, and it ain't human for anybody to give up two thousand dollars for that forty-pound chunk of freckled wildcat. I'm willing to take a chance at fifteen hundred dollars. You can charge the difference up to me."

So, to relieve Bill, I agreed, and we wrote a letter that was something like this:

To: Mr. Ebenezer Dorset of Summit
Mr. Ebenezer Dorset:
We have your boy **concealed**[20] in a place far from Summit. It is useless for you or the most

---

[19] **strutted**—walked with stiff steps, chest out, and shoulders back.
[20] **concealed**—hidden.

skillful detectives to try to find him. Absolutely the only terms on which you can have him brought back to you are these: We demand fifteen hundred dollars in large bills for his return. The money should be left at midnight tonight at the same spot and in the same box as your reply, as described below. If you agree to these terms, send your answer in writing by a messenger tonight at 8:30 p.m.

After crossing Owl Creek, on the road to Poplar Cove, there are three large trees about a hundred yards apart, close to the fence of the wheat field on the right-hand side. At the bottom of the fencepost, opposite the third tree, will be found a small cardboard box. The messenger will place the answer in this box and return immediately to Summit.

If you contact the police or fail to meet our demands as stated, you will never see your boy again. If you pay the money, he will be returned to you safe and well within three hours. These terms are final, and if you do not agree to them, no further communication will be attempted.

TWO DESPERATE MEN

I addressed this letter to Dorset and put it in my pocket. As I was about to leave, the kid comes up to me and says:

"Aw, Snake-eye, you said I could play the Black Scout while you was gone."

"Play it, of course," says I. "Mr. Bill will play with you. What kind of a game is it?"

"I'm the Black Scout," says Red Chief, "and I have to ride to the **stockade**[21] to warn the settlers that the Indians are coming. I'm tired of playing Indian myself. I want to be the Black Scout."

"All right," says I. "It sounds harmless to me. I guess Mr. Bill will play with you."

"What am I supposed to do?" asks Bill, looking at the kid suspiciously.

"You are the horse," says Black Scout. "Get down on your hands and knees. How can I ride to the stockade without a hoss?"

"You'd better keep him interested," I said, "till we get the **scheme**[22] going. Loosen up."

Bill gets down on all fours, and a look comes in his eye like a rabbit's when you catch it in a trap.

"How far is it to the stockade, kid?" he asks, in a hoarse voice.

"Ninety miles," says the Black Scout. "And you have to move it if you want to get there on time. Whoa, now!"

---

[21] **stockade**—fort; enclosed area.

[22] **scheme**—plan.

The Black Scout jumps on Bill's back and digs his heels in his side.

"For Heaven's sake," says Bill, "hurry back, Sam, as soon as you can. I wish we hadn't made the ransom more than a thousand. Say, kid, you quit kicking me or I'll get up and spank you good."

I walked over to Poplar Cove and sat around the post office and store, talking with the people that came in to trade. One old man says that he hears Summit is all upset on account of Ebenezer Dorset's boy having been lost or stolen. That was all I wanted to know. I bought some smoking tobacco, made a comment about the price of black-eyed peas, mailed my letter secretly, and then left. The postmaster said the mail carrier would come by in an hour to take the mail on to Summit.

When I got back to the cave, Bill and the boy were not to be found.

When I got back to the cave, Bill and the boy were not to be found. I looked in the area near the cave, and risked a yell or two, but there was no response. So I lighted my pipe and sat down on a moss-covered rock to await developments.

In about half an hour, I heard the bushes rustle, and Bill crawled out into the little clearing in front of the cave. Behind him was the kid, stepping softly like a scout, with a broad grin on his face. Bill stopped, took off his hat and wiped his face with a red handkerchief. The kid stopped about eight feet behind him.

"Sam," says Bill, "I suppose you'll think I'm a complainer, but I can't help it. I'm a grown man with a strong body and a strong mind, but there is a point that even I must say 'no more.' The boy is gone. I sent him home. The whole scheme is off. I couldn't stand another minute of it. I tried to stay faithful to our plan, but I just couldn't."

"What's the trouble, Bill?" I asks him.

"I was rode," says Bill, "the ninety miles to the stockade. Then, when the settlers were rescued, I was given oats to eat, and they tasted as awful as sand on the beach. And then, for an hour I had to try to explain to him why there was nothin' in holes, how a road can run both ways, and what makes the grass green. I tell you, Sam, a human can only stand so much. I takes him by the neck of his clothes and drags him down the mountain. On the way, he kicks my legs black-and-blue from the knees down, and I've got two or three bites on my thumb and hand.

"But he's gone"—continues Bill—"he's gone home. I showed him the road to Summit and kicked him about eight feet nearer to home. I'm sorry we

lose the ransom; but it was either that or take Bill
Driscoll to the madhouse."

Bill is puffing and blowing, but there is a look of
peace and contentment on his face.

"Bill," says I, "there isn't any heart disease in
your family, is there?"

"No," says Bill, "Why?"

"Then maybe you should turn around," says I,
"and have a look behind you."

Bill turns and sees the boy, and he goes pale and
sits down hard on the ground and begins to pick
quietly at grass and little sticks. For an hour I was
afraid for his mind. And then I told him that
my scheme was to put the whole job through
immediately. We would get the ransom and be off
with it by midnight if old Dorset agreed to what we
said in the letter. So Bill pulled himself together
enough to give the kid a weak sort
of smile. He even promised to play the Russian
in a Japanese war with him as soon as he felt a
little better.

I had a plan for collecting that ransom without
danger of being caught. The tree under which
Dorset's answer was to be left—and the money
later on—was close to the road fence with big, bare

fields on all sides. If a gang of constables should be watching for anyone to come for the note, they would be able to see him a long way off crossing the fields or in the road. But no, sir! At half-past eight, I was up in that tree as well hidden as a tree toad, waiting for the messenger to arrive.

Exactly on time, a half-grown boy rides up the road on a bicycle, locates the cardboard box at the foot of the fence post, slips a folded piece of paper into it, and pedals away again back toward Summit.

I waited an hour and then decided that all was clear. I slid down the tree, got the note, slipped along the fence till I reached the woods, and was back at the cave in another half an hour. I opened the note, got near the lantern, and read it to Bill. It was written with a pen in small writing, and it went like this:

> To: Two Desperate Men
> Gentlemen,
>
> I received your letter today by mail and read your request for ransom in return for my son. I think you are a little high in your demands, so I will make you a counteroffer[23] which I believe you may decide to accept. You bring Johnny home and pay me two hundred and fifty dollars in cash,

---

[23] counteroffer—proposal in return.

and I will take him off your hands. You had better come at night, for the neighbors believe he is lost, and I couldn't be responsible for what they would do to anybody they saw bringing him back.

Very respectfully,
Ebenezer Dorset

"Well, for heaven sakes!" says I, "of all the **impudent**—"[24]

But I glanced at Bill, and hesitated. He had the most appealing look in his eyes I ever saw on the face of an animal or a person.

"Sam," says he, "what's two hundred and fifty dollars, after all? We've got the money. One more night of this kid will send me to a bed in Bedlam.[25] Besides being a thorough gentleman, I think Mr. Dorset is making us a fine offer. You ain't going to let the chance go, are you?"

"Tell you the truth, Bill," says I, "this little lamb has somewhat got on my nerves too. We'll take him home, pay the ransom, and make our getaway."

We took him home that night. We got him to go by telling him that his father had bought a silver-mounted rifle and a pair of moccasins for him, and we were going to hunt bears the next day.

---

[24] **impudent**—bold and cocky.
[25] Bedlam—a famous hospital for the insane in London.

It was just midnight when we knocked at Ebenezer's front door. Just at the moment when I should have been taking the fifteen hundred dollars from the box under the tree, according to the original plan, Bill was counting out two hundred and fifty dollars into Dorset's hand.

When the kid found out we were going to leave him at home, he started up a howl and fastened himself as tight as a **leech**[26] to Bill's leg. His father peeled him away as best he could.

"How long can you hold him?" asks Bill.

"I'm not as strong as I used to be," says old Dorset, "but I think I can promise you ten minutes."

"Enough," says Bill. "In ten minutes I shall cross the Central, Southern and Middle Western States, and be heading straight for the Canadian border."

And, even though it was dark, and as fat as Bill was and as good a runner as I am, he was a good mile and a half out of Summit before I could catch up with him.

THE END

---

[26] **leech**—blood-sucking worm.

Friends and Neighbors

One Thousand Dollars

Young Robert Gillian inherits one thousand dollars.
How will he decide to spend it?

"One thousand dollars," repeated Lawyer Tolman, seriously. "Here is your money."

Young Gillian gave an amused laugh as he thumbed through the thin package of new fifty-dollar bills. "It's such a strange amount," he explained, in a friendly voice, to the lawyer. "If it had been ten thousand, a fellow might wind up with a lot of fireworks and have a good time. Even fifty dollars would have been less trouble."

"You heard the reading of your uncle's **will**,"[1] continued Lawyer Tolman, in a dry tone of voice. "I don't know if you paid much attention to its details. I must remind you of one. As soon as you have spent the money, you are required to give us an exact account of how you spent this $1,000. The will makes that clear. I trust that you will agree to the late[2] Mr. Gillian's wishes."

"You can count on it," said the young man, politely. "I might have to find a secretary. I was never good at accounts."

After leaving the law firm, Gillian went to his club. There he looked for a man he called Old Bryson.

Old Bryson, a calm, forty-year-old man, was sitting quietly in the corner reading a book. When he saw Gillian approaching, he sighed, laid down his book, and took off his glasses.

"Old Bryson, wake up," said Gillian. "I have a funny story to tell you."

"I wish you would tell it to someone in the billiards[3] room," said Old Bryson. "You know how I hate your stories."

"This is a better one than usual," said Gillian, rolling a cigarette, "and I'm glad to tell it to you. It's

---

[1] **will**—legal document that tells what to do with a person's property after he or she is dead.

[2] late—dead.

[3] billiards—game similar to pool.

too sad and funny to tell in the billiards room. I've just come from my late uncle's law firm. The old man left me an even thousand dollars in his will. Now, what can a man possibly do with a thousand dollars?"

"I thought," said Old Bryson, showing as much interest as a bee shows in a bowl of vinegar, "that the late Septimus Gillian was worth something like half a million dollars."

"He was," agreed Gillian, joyously, "and that's where the joke comes in. He's left his whole fortune to a germ. That is, part of it goes to the man who discovers a new germ and the rest to establish a hospital that will do away with it again.

"However, the butler and the housekeeper get a ring and $10 each. I get $1,000."

"You've always had plenty of money to spend," observed Old Bryson.

"Correct," said Gillian. "My uncle was like a fairy godmother when it came to my allowance."

"Any other **heirs**?"[4] asked Old Bryson.

"None." Gillian frowned at his cigarette and kicked a leather sofa nervously. "There is a Miss Hayden, a ward[5] of my uncle, who lived in his house. She's a quiet thing, musical, the daughter of somebody who was unlucky enough to be my uncle's

---

[4] **heirs**—people who inherit money or property after a death.
[5] ward—person who is legally under the care of another.

friend. I forgot to say that she was in on the seal ring and $10 joke, too. I wish I had been. Then I could have had two bottles of wine, tipped the waiter with the ring, and had the whole business off my hands. Don't be snobbish and rude, Old Bryson—tell me what I can do with a thousand dollars."

Old Bryson rubbed his glasses and smiled. And when Old Bryson smiled, Gillian knew that he intended to be ruder than ever.

"A thousand dollars," he said, "means much or little. One man may buy a happy home with it and laugh at Rockefeller.[6] Another could send his wife South with it and save her life. A thousand dollars would buy pure milk for one hundred babies during June, July, and August and save fifty of their lives. You could count upon a half hour's amusement gambling. It would provide an education to a smart boy. I am told that a genuine Corot[7] was bought for that amount in an auction room yesterday. You could move to a New Hampshire town and live respectably two years on it. You could rent Madison Square Garden[8] for one evening with it and lecture your audience, if you should have one, on what it's like to be the heir of a wealthy man."

---

[6] Rockefeller—John D. Rockefeller (1839–1937), at the time one of the wealthiest men in the world.

[7] Corot—painting by Jean Baptiste Corot (1796–1875), a French painter.

[8] Madison Square Garden—large stadium in New York.

"People might like you, Old Bryson," said Gillian, almost without irritation, "if you wouldn't preach so much. I asked you to tell me what I could do with a thousand dollars."

"You?" said Bryson, with a gentle laugh. "Why, Bobby Gillian, there's only one logical thing you could do. You can go buy Miss Lotta Lauriere a diamond necklace with the money and then move to Idaho and put yourself on a ranch of some type. I advise a sheep ranch, as I have a particular dislike for sheep."

"Thanks," said Gillian, rising. "I thought I could depend upon you, Old Bryson. You hit on an excellent plan. I wanted to get rid of the money in a lump because I've got to turn in an account for it, and I hate working with numbers."

Gillian phoned for a cab and said to the driver:

"The stage entrance of the Columbine Theater."

Miss Lotta Lauriere was helping nature by powdering her face when Gillian arrived. "Let it in," said Miss Lauriere when her dresser, Miss Adams, announced that Gillian was at the door.

"Now, what is it, Bobby? I'm going on in two minutes."

"Put a little powder on your right ear," suggested Gillian, critically. "That's better. It won't take two minutes for me. What would you say about a necklace as a gift? I can afford three zeros with a one in front of them."

"Oh, whatever you say, Bobby," said Miss Lauriere distractedly. "I need my right glove, Adams. Say, Bobby, did you see that necklace Della Stacey had on the other night? Twenty-two hundred dollars it cost at Tiffany's.[9] But, of course—pull my sash a little to the left, Adams."

"Miss Lauriere, they need you on stage!" cried a voice in the hall.

Gillian walked slowly out to where his cab was waiting.

"What would you do with a thousand dollars if you had it?" he asked the driver.

"Open a saloon," said the cabby promptly and hoarsely. "I know a place I could take money in with both hands. It's a four-story brick on a corner. I've got it figured out. Second floor, Chinese restaurant—third floor, manicure shop—fourth floor, a poolroom. If you was thinking of putting up the money—"

"Oh, no," said Gillian, "I was just curious. I'll have a ride with you, though. Drive till I tell you to stop."

---

[9] Tiffany's—famous jewelry store.

Eight blocks down Broadway, Gillian got out again and told the cab driver to wait. A blind man sat upon a stool on the sidewalk selling pencils. Gillian went out and stood before him.

"Excuse me," he said, "but would you mind telling me what you would do if you had a thousand dollars?"

"You got out of that cab that just drove up, didn't you?" asked the blind man.

"I did," said Gillian.

"Then I guess you're all right," said the pencil dealer, "if you can afford to ride in a cab in the daylight. Take a look at that, if you like."

He pulled a small book from his coat pocket and held it out. Gillian opened it and saw that it was a bank deposit book. It showed a balance of $1,785 to the blind man's credit.

Gillian returned the book and got into the cab.

"I forgot something," he said. "You may drive to the law offices of Tolman & Sharp, on Broadway."

When Gillian got there, Lawyer Tolman stared at him through his gold-rimmed glasses. Clearly the lawyer was not happy to see Gillian again.

"I beg your pardon," said Gillian, cheerfully, "but may I ask you a question? It is not a rude one, I hope. Was Miss Hayden left anything by my uncle's will besides the ring and the $10?"

"Nothing," said Mr. Tolman.

"I thank you very much, sir," said Gillian, and he went back out to his cab. He gave the driver the address of his late uncle's home.

Miss Hayden was writing letters in the library. She was small and slender and clothed in black. But you would have noticed her eyes. Gillian drifted in and stood leaning on her desk.

"I've just come from old Tolman's," he explained. "They've been going over the papers down there. They found a"—Gillian searched his memory for a legal term—"they found an **amendment**[10] or a codicil[11] or something to the will. It seemed that the old boy loosened up a little at the end and willed you a thousand dollars. I was driving up this way and Tolman asked me to bring you the money. Here it is. You'd better count it to see if it's right." Gillian laid the money beside her hand on the desk.

Miss Hayden turned white. "Oh!" she said, and again, "Oh!"

Gillian half turned and looked out of the window.

She was small and slender and clothed in black. But you would have noticed her eyes.

---

[10] **amendment**—correction.

[11] codicil—document that changes an earlier will.

"I suppose, of course," he said, in a low voice, "that you know I love you."

"I am sorry," said Miss Hayden, taking up her money.

"There is no use?" asked Gillian, almost light-heartedly.

"I am sorry," she said again.

"May I write a note?" asked Gillian, with a smile. He seated himself at the big library table. She supplied him with paper and pen, and then went back to her letters.

Gillian wrote his account of the thousand dollars in these words:

"Paid by the black sheep,[12] Robert Gillian, $1,000 on account of the everlasting happiness owed by Heaven to the best and dearest woman on Earth."

Gillian slipped his writing into an envelope, bowed and went his way.

His cab stopped again at the offices of Tolman & Sharp.

"I have spent the thousand dollars," he said cheerfully, to Tolman of the gold glasses, "and I have come to give you an account of it, as I agreed. There is quite a feeling of summer in the air—don't you think so, Mr. Tolman?" He tossed a white envelope

---

[12] black sheep—member of the family who is considered to be not respectable.

on the lawyer's table. "You will find there a memo, sir, that explains how I spent the money."

Without touching the envelope, Mr. Tolman went to a door and called his partner, Mr. Sharp. Together they explored the inside of a large safe. Eventually they pulled out a big envelope sealed with wax. This they forcibly opened, and shook their heads together after reading its contents. Then Tolman became spokesman.

"Mr. Gillian," he said, formally, "there was a codicil to your uncle's will. He gave us this codicil privately, with instructions not to open it until you had given us a full accounting of the $1,000. Since you have done this, my partner and I have read the codicil. I don't want to confuse you with the legal words, so I'll simply tell you what it says.

"Your uncle said that if you spend the money in a way that is careful, wise, and generous, then you will be rewarded with the sum of $50,000. Mr. Sharp and I are to be the judge of whether you have spent wisely, and I promise you that we will be fair.

"If, on the other hand, Mr. Gillian, you have spent the money as you have spent it in the past—on gambling, drinking, or some such foolishness—the $50,000 is to be paid to Miriam Hayden, ward of the late Mr. Gillian, without delay. Now, Mr. Gillian, Mr. Sharp and I will examine your account to see how you spent the $1,000."

Mr. Tolman reached for the envelope, but Gillian was a little quicker in picking it up. He tore the envelope and the paper inside into tiny strips and dropped them into his pocket.

"It's all right," he said, smilingly. "You don't need to bother reading this. I don't suppose you'd understand these bets, anyway. I lost the thousand dollars at the races. Good-day to you, gentlemen."

Tolman & Sharp shook their heads sadly at each other when Gillian left, for they heard him whistling happily in the hallway as he waited for the elevator.

THE END

The Last Leaf

An artist named Johnsy lies dying in her bed. Because she is so weak, all she can do is stare out the window and watch leaves drop from a vine. When the last leaf falls, Johnsy decides, she will die.

In a little district west of New York City's Washington Square, the streets have run crazy and broken themselves into small strips called "places." These "places" make strange angles and curves. One street crosses itself a time or two. An artist once thought of a valuable possibility in this street. Suppose a collector with a bill for paints, paper, and canvas[1] should, in walking this route, suddenly

---

[1] canvas—a piece of woven cloth to paint on.

meet himself coming back, without having collected a cent on the accounts!

So, to old Greenwich Village[2] the art people soon came. They hunted for north-facing windows and interesting buildings with lofts and low rents. When there were enough artists there, they became a "colony."

At the top of a small, three-story brick building, Sue and Johnsy had their art studio. "Johnsy" was a nickname for Joanna. Sue was from Maine; and Johnsy was from California. They had met at a table in Delmonico's restaurant and discovered that their tastes in art, salad, and art overalls were so similar that they decided to rent a studio together.

That was in May. In November, a cold, unseen stranger that the doctors called **pneumonia**[3] stalked about the colony, touching one here and there with his icy fingers. On the east side of the colony, this invader walked boldly, striking down his victims by the score.[4] But he was forced to slow down a bit when he got to the narrow streets and alleyways of the "places."

---

[2] Greenwich Village—New York City neighborhood around Washington Square.

[3] **pneumonia**—disease of the lungs that killed many people before the invention of penicillin.

[4] by the score—in large numbers. A score is twenty.

Mr. Pneumonia was not what you would call a kindly old gentleman. A tiny woman with blood that has been thinned by warm sunshine and California breezes was no match for his cruel games. But soon he touched Johnsy with his icy fingers. She lay, scarcely moving, on her painted iron bedstead, looking through the small Dutch window-panes at the blank side of the brick house next door.

> *"Johnsy has one chance in—let us say, ten," he said, as he shook down his thermometer. "And that chance depends on her will to live."*

One morning, the busy doctor called Sue into the hallway. "Johnsy has one chance in—let us say, ten," he said, as he shook down his thermometer. "And that chance depends on her will to live. Your friend has made up her mind that she's not going to get well. Is there anything on her mind?"

"Well, she—she wanted to paint the Bay of Naples[5] some day," said Sue.

"Paint?—bosh! Does she have anything on her mind that's worth thinking about—a man, for instance?"

---

[5] Bay of Naples—body of water in Italy.

"A man?" said Sue, with some anger. "Is a man worth—but, no, doctor; there is no man in her life."

"Well, the disease will run its course, then," said the doctor. "I will do all that I can with my medicine. But whenever a patient begins to count the carriages in her funeral procession,[6] medicine loses half its value. If you will get her to ask one question about the new winter styles in coat sleeves, I will promise you a one-in-five chance for her, instead of one-in-ten."

After the doctor had gone, Sue went into the workroom and cried. Then she put on a cheerful face, started to whistle, and walked into Johnsy's room with her drawing board in hand.

Johnsy lay, scarcely making a ripple under the bedclothes, with her face toward the window. Sue stopped whistling, thinking she was asleep.

Sue arranged her board and began a pen-and-ink drawing that would be used to illustrate a magazine story. Young artists must pave their way to Art by drawing pictures for magazine stories that young authors must write to pave their way to Literature.

As Sue was sketching a pair of elegant horseshow riding pants and a monocle[7] on the figure of the hero,

---

[6] begins . . . procession—starts to imagine her funeral.

[7] monocle—an eyeglass for one eye.

an Idaho cowboy, she heard a low sound, several times repeated. She went quickly to the bedside.

Johnsy's eyes were open wide. She was looking out the window and counting—counting backward.

"Twelve," she said, and a little later "eleven," and then "ten," and "nine"—and then "eight" and "seven," almost together.

Sue looked carefully out the window. What was Johnsy counting? Sue could only see a bare, dreary yard and the blank side of the brick house twenty feet away. An old, old ivy vine, **gnarled**[8] and decayed at the roots, climbed halfway up the brick wall. The cold breath of autumn had made the leaves fall from the vine until its skeleton branches clung, almost bare, to the crumbling bricks.

"What is it, dear?" asked Sue.

"Six," said Johnsy, in almost a whisper. "They're falling faster now. Three days ago there were almost a hundred. It made my head ache to count them. But now it's easy. There goes another one. There are only five left now."

"Five what, dear? Tell your Sudie."

"Leaves. On the ivy vine. When the last one falls I must go, too. I've known that for three days. Didn't the doctor tell you?"

---

[8] **gnarled**—twisted; knotty.

"Oh, I never heard of such nonsense," said Sue, with wonderful energy. "What do old ivy leaves have to do with your getting well? And you used to love that vine so much, you naughty girl. Don't be silly. Why, the doctor told me this morning that your chances for getting well real soon were—let's see exactly what he said—he said the chances were ten to one! Why, that's almost as good a chance as we have in New York when we ride on the street cars or walk past a new building. Try to take some soup now, and let Sudie go back to her drawing, so she can sell it to the editor, and buy port wine[9] for her sick child, and pork chops for her greedy self."

"You don't need to get any more wine," said Johnsy, keeping her eyes fixed out the window. "There goes another. And no, I don't want any soup. Now there are just four leaves left. I want to see the last one fall before it gets dark. Then I'll go, too."

"Johnsy, dear," said Sue, bending over her, "will you promise me to keep your eyes closed, and not look out the window until I am done working? I must hand these drawings in by tomorrow. I need the light, or I would draw with the shade down."

"Couldn't you draw in the other room?" asked Johnsy, coldly.

---

[9] port wine—sweet red wine.

"I'd rather be here by you," said Sue. "Besides, I don't want you to keep looking at those silly ivy leaves."

"Let me know as soon as you have finished," said Johnsy, closing her eyes and lying white and still as a fallen statue, "because I want to see the last one fall. I'm tired of waiting. I'm tired of thinking. I want to turn loose my hold on everything and go sailing down, down, just like one of those poor, tired leaves."

"Try to sleep," said Sue. "I must ask Mr. Behrman to come up to be my model for the old miner. I'll only be gone for a minute. Don't try to move 'til I come back."

Mr. Behrman was a painter who lived on the ground floor beneath them. He was past sixty and had a long white beard that curled down past his **stooped**[10] shoulders. Behrman was a failure in art. For forty years he had painted without any success. He had always been about to paint a masterpiece but had never yet begun it. For several years, he painted nothing except things that he could sell to a magazine or an advertising agency. He earned a little money by serving as a model for young artists in the colony who could not pay the price of a professional.

---

[10] **stooped**—bent.

He drank a great deal of gin and still talked about his coming masterpiece. For the rest of the time, he was a fierce little old man, who made terrible fun of softness in anyone. Even so, he had a warm place in his heart for the two young artists upstairs, and he considered it his job to protect them.

He was a fierce little old man, who made terrible fun of softness in anyone.

Sue found Behrman smelling strongly of gin in his dimly lighted den below. In one corner was a blank canvas on an easel that had been waiting there for twenty-five years to receive the first line of the masterpiece. She told him of Johnsy's illness and how she was convinced that she would let herself float away when the last ivy leaf fluttered to the ground.

Old Behrman, his red eyes wet with tears, shouted his disgust for such foolish ideas.

"What!" he cried. "Are there people in the world with the foolishness to die because leaves drop off a darn vine? I have not heard of such a thing. No, I will not pose as a model for your fool miner. Why did you allow dat[11] silly business to come into her head? Ach, the poor leetle Miss Yohnsy."

---

[11] dat—that.

"She is very ill and weak," said Sue, "and the fever has left her mind full of strange ideas. Very well, Mr. Behrman, if you don't want to pose for me, you don't have to. But I think you are a horrible old—old flibbertigibbet."[12]

"You are just like a woman I once knew!" yelled Behrman. "Who said I will not pose? Go on. I come wit' you. For half an hour I have been trying to say that I am ready to pose! What kind of world is this if someone as good as Miss Yohnsy can be so sick? Someday I will paint a masterpiece, and we shall all go away! Yes, I will!"

Johnsy was sleeping when they went upstairs. Sue pulled the shade down to the windowsill, and motioned Behrman into the other room. In there they peered out the window fearfully at the ivy vine. Then they looked at each other for a moment without speaking. A steady, cold rain was falling, mingled with snow. Behrman, in his old blue shirt, took a seat and posed as an old miner.

* * *

When Sue awoke from an hour's sleep the next morning, she found Johnsy with dull, wide-open eyes staring at the drawn green shade.

---

[12] flibbertigibbet—silly, scatterbrained person.

"Pull it up. I want to see," she ordered, in a whisper.

Wearily Sue obeyed.

But look! Even after the beating rain and fierce wind that lasted all night, there still remained one last leaf on the ivy vine. The leaf was dark green near its stem, but its edges were tinted with the yellow of decay. It hung bravely from a branch some twenty feet above the ground.

"It is the last one," said Johnsy. "I thought it would surely fall during the night. I heard the wind. It will fall today, and I shall die at the same time."

"Dear, dear!" said Sue, leaning her worn face down to the pillow, "think of me, if you won't think of yourself. What would I do without you?"

But Johnsy did not answer. The most lonely thing in all the world is a soul when it is getting ready to go on its mysterious, far journey. Johnsy felt that her friendship with Sue was not nearly as important as preparing herself to die.

The day wore away, and even through the **twilight**[13] they could see the lone ivy leaf clinging to its stem against the wall. And then, with the coming of the night, the north wind began blowing again.

---

[13] **twilight**—half light of late afternoon or early evening.

The rain still beat hard against the window and pattered down from the roof.

When it was light enough, Johnsy, the **merciless**,[14] commanded that the shade be raised.

The ivy leaf was still there.

Johnsy lay for a long time looking at it. Then she called to Sue, who was stirring some chicken broth over the gas stove.

"I've been a bad girl, Sudie," said Johnsy. "Something has made that last leaf stay there to show me how wicked I was. It is a sin to want to die. You may bring me a little broth now, and some milk with a little wine in it. No, bring me a mirror first, and then pack some pillows about me. Then I can sit up and watch you cook.

"I've been a bad girl, Sudie," said Johnsy

An hour later Johnsy said: "Sudie, some day I hope to paint the Bay of Naples."

The doctor came in the afternoon, and Sue made an excuse to go into the hallway as he left.

"The chances are even now that she'll live," said the doctor, smiling. "With good nursing, you'll win. And now I must see another case I have downstairs. Behrman, his name is—some kind of an artist, I believe. He has pneumonia, too. He is an old, weak

---

[14] **merciless**—without mercy; unsympathetic.

man, and the attack is very bad. There is no hope for him; but he goes to the hospital today to be made more comfortable."

The next day the doctor said to Sue: "She's out of danger. You've won. Good food and care now— that's all."

That afternoon Sue came to the bed where Johnsy lay, contentedly knitting a very blue and very useless scarf, and put one arm around her, pillows and all.

"I have something to tell you, white mouse," she said. "Mr. Behrman died of pneumonia today in the hospital. He was ill only two days. The janitor found him the day before yesterday in his room, helpless with pain. His shoes and clothing were wet through and icy cold. They couldn't imagine where he had been on such a terrible night. And then they found a lantern, still lighted, and a ladder that had been dragged from its place, and some scattered brushes, and an artist's board with green and yellow colors mixed on it, and—look out the window, dear, at the last ivy leaf on the wall. Didn't you wonder why it never fluttered or moved when the wind blew? Ah, darling, it's Behrman's masterpiece—he painted it there the night that the last leaf fell."

THE END

The Third Ingredient

Hetty Pepper has no money to buy potatoes and an onion for her beef stew. It's amazing what can happen when you need potatoes and an onion.

The Vallambrosa apartment house is not really an apartment house. It is two old-fashioned houses that were joined together to make one. A room at the Vallambrosa might cost you two dollars a week, or it might cost you twenty dollars, depending on what the room looked like. Among the Vallambrosa's roomers[1] are secretaries, musicians, bank clerks, shopgirls, writers, art students, wiretappers, and other people who lean far over the **banister**[2] rail when the doorbell rings.

---

[1] roomers—people who rent rooms to live in.

[2] **banister**—handrail on the stairs.

This story is about just two of the Vallambrosians—though no disrespect is meant to the others.

At six o'clock one afternoon, Hetty Pepper came back to her third-floor rear, $3.50 room in the Vallambrosa. Her nose and chin were more sharply pointed than usual. To be fired from the department store where you have been working for four years, with only fifteen cents in your purse, would be likely to make anyone's chin and nose look a little sharper.

And now for Hetty's short **biography**[3] while she climbs the two flights of stairs.

Hetty had walked into the Biggest Department Store one morning four years before, with seventy-five other girls. All of them were applying for a job in the shirt and blouse department. The group of seventy-five wage-earners made a scene of confusing beauty. The scene was all the more remarkable because every woman there—except Hetty—was so amazingly, brilliantly blonde.

A trustworthy, cool-eyed, baldheaded young man had the job of hiring one of the women. He felt as if he was in a sea of yellow taffy, while white

---

[3] **biography**—life story.

hand-embroidered[4] clouds floated around him. Then his eyes landed on a rescue boat. Hetty Pepper, a plain-of-face woman with small, scornful green eyes and chocolate-colored hair. She was dressed in a plain suit and a common-sense hat and stood before him looking every one of her full twenty-nine years.

"You're hired!" shouted the baldheaded young man and was saved. That is how Hetty came to be employed in the Biggest Department Store. The story of her rise to an eight-dollar-a-week salary is the combined stories of Hercules, Joan of Arc,[5] Job,[6] and Little Red Riding Hood.

The story of Hetty's firing from the Biggest Department Store is so similar to the story of her hiring that it is almost boring.

In each department of the store there is an **omnipresent**[7] and **omnivorous**[8] person who always wears a red tie and is called a "buyer." The future of the girls in his department is in his hands. He makes the decision to hire—and fire—each and every employee.

This particular buyer was a trustworthy, cool-eyed, baldheaded young man. As he walked along

---

[4] hand-embroidered—decorated with needlework done by hand.

[5] Joan of Arc—French heroine (1412–1431) who led armies against the English.

[6] Job—in the Bible, a very patient man who kept his faith in God despite many troubles.

[7] **omnipresent**—always there.

[8] **omnivorous**—eating everything.

the aisles of his department, he seemed to be sailing on a sea of yellow taffy, with white clouds, machine-embroidered, all around him. Tired by the taste of the taffy, he looked upon Hetty Pepper's plain face, green eyes, and chocolate-colored hair as a welcome relief in this sea of sticky-sweet beauty. In a quiet corner of the departments, he pinched her arm kindly, three inches above the elbow. She slapped him three feet away with one good blow of her muscular and not especially lily-white right hand. So, now you know why Hetty Pepper came to leave the Biggest Department Store at thirty minutes notice, with one dime and a nickel in her purse.

She slapped him three feet away with one good blow of her muscular and not especially lily-white right hand.

There's one other thing you must know before we can return to Hetty, who is still on the stairs. In this morning's newspaper, the price of rib beef is six cents per pound. But on the day that Hetty was "released" by the department store, the price was seven and a half cents per pound. That fact is what makes this story possible. Otherwise, the extra three cents would have—

* * *

Hetty climbed the stairs to her apartment with her two pounds of beef. Her purse was empty. However, after a hot, delicious beef stew for supper and a night's good sleep, she would be fit in the morning to apply again for jobs.

In her room, Hetty got the stoneware stew-pan out of the two-by-four-foot china—er—I mean stoneware—closet and began to dig down in a rat's-nest of paper bags for the potatoes and onions. She came out with her nose and chin just a little sharper pointed.

There was neither a potato nor an onion. Now, what kind of a beef stew can you make out of simply beef? You can make oyster soup without oysters, turtle soup without turtles, coffee cake without coffee, but you can't make beef stew without potatoes and onions. But beef alone, with salt and pepper and a tablespoon of flour, first stirred in a little cold water, will serve.

Hetty took her saucepan to the rear of the third-floor hall. According to the advertisements of the Vallambrosa, running water was to be found there. Between you and me and the water meter, the water only **ambled**[9] or walked through the faucets,

---

[9] **ambled**—walked slowly, as if with no purpose.

but we can't be concerned with that problem here. Hetty made her way to the sink in the back, where many of the Vallambrosa's roomers often met to dump out their coffee grounds and stare at one another's **kimonos**.[10]

At this sink, Hetty found a girl with heavy, gold-brown, artistic hair and sad eyes, who was washing two large white potatoes. Hetty knew the roomers in the Vallambrosa as well as anyone else did. She knew that the girl with the potatoes was a painter who specialized in **miniatures**.[11] She lived in a kind of attic—or "studio," as the Vallambrosa preferred to call it—on the top floor. Hetty was not certain in her mind what a miniature was; it certainly wasn't a house. House painters, although they wear splashy overalls and poke ladders in your face on the street, are known to have all kinds of food at home.

The potato girl was quite slim and small, and she handled her potatoes like an old **bachelor**[12] uncle handles a baby who is teething. She had a dull shoemaker's knife in her right hand, and she had begun to peel one of the potatoes with it.

---

[10] **kimonos**—robes.

[11] **miniatures**—very small portraits or paintings.

[12] **bachelor**—unmarried man.

Hetty said, in her usual formal tone of voice: "Beg pardon for butting into what's not my business, but if you peel them potatoes, you lose out. What you want to do is *scrape* 'em. Let me show you."

She took a potato and the knife, and began to demonstrate.

"Oh, thank you," breathed the artist. "I didn't know. And I *did* hate to see the thick peeling go. It seemed like such a waste. But I thought they always had to be peeled. When you've got only potatoes to eat, the peelings count, you know."

"Say, kid," said Hetty, holding her knife, "you having a hard time, too, are you?"

The miniature artist smiled hungrily.

"I suppose I am. Art—or, at least, my type of art—doesn't seem to be much in demand. I have only these potatoes for my dinner. But they aren't so bad boiled and hot, with a little butter and salt."

"Child," said Hetty, letting a brief smile soften her sharp features, "Fate has sent me and you together. I've had it handed to me in the neck,[13] too, but I've got a chunk of meat in my room as big as a lapdog. And I've done everything to get potatoes except pray for 'em. Let's me and you put our food together and make a stew. We'll cook it in my room. If we only had an onion to go in it! Say, kid, you

---

[13] had it handed to me in the neck—been given bad luck.

haven't got a couple of pennies that've slipped down into the lining of your winter jacket, have you? I could run down to the corner and get one at old Giuseppe's stand. A stew without an onion is worse than a movie without candy.

"You may call me Cecilia," said the artist. "No, I spent my last penny three days ago."

"Then we'll have to cut the onion out instead of slicing it in," said Hetty. "I'd ask the janitor for one, but I don't want him to know just yet that I'm out of a job. But I wish we did have an onion."

In Hetty's room, the two began to prepare their supper. Cecilia's job was to sit on the couch helplessly and beg to be allowed to do something, in the voice of a cooing dove. Hetty prepared the rib beef, putting it in cold salted water in the saucepan and setting it on the one-burner gas stove.

"I wish we had an onion," said Hetty, as she scraped the two potatoes.

On the wall opposite Hetty's couch was a gorgeous advertisement of one of the new ferryboats of the P.U.F.F. Railroad that had been built to cut down the time between Los Angeles and New York City one-eighth of a minute.

Hetty, turning her head as she spoke, saw tears running from her guest's eyes as she gazed on the picture of the sleek, fast ferryboat.

"Why, say, Cecilia, kid," said Hetty, holding her knife, "is the picture as bad as that? I ain't an art critic, but I thought it kind of brightened up the room. Of course, a manicure[14] painter could tell it was a bad picture in a minute. I'll take it down if you say so. I wish to the holy Saint Potluck we had an onion."

> *She had accepted her role long ago. She was a shoulder to lean on— someone to help those in need.*

But the miniature painter had tumbled down, sobbing, with her nose pressing into the hard-woven cloth of the couch. Something was wrong here, and it must be more than an artist upset by a bad picture.

Hetty knew. She had accepted her role long ago. She was a shoulder to lean on—someone to help those in need, which was certainly the case with the little artist. Although Hetty's shoulder was sharp and lean, all her life people had laid their heads there and had left all or half of their troubles. In all the world, there were few collarbones as sturdy and trustworthy as hers.

Hetty was only thirty-three, so she still felt a little pang whenever a head of youth and beauty leaned

---

[14] Hetty means *miniature*, a small painting; *manicure* means treatment of the hands and nails.

upon her for help. But one glance in her mirror always served as an instant painkiller. So she gave one pale look into the old mirror on the wall above the gas stove and turned down the flame a little lower from the bubbling beef and potatoes. Hetty went over to the couch and lifted Cecilia's head to rest upon her shoulder.

"Go on and tell me, honey," she said. "I know now that it ain't art that's worrying you. Let me guess: You met a man on a ferryboat, didn't you? Go on, Cecilia, kid, and tell your—your Aunt Hetty about it."

After another bucket of tears flowed, the artist finally told her story. "It was only three days ago. I was coming back on the ferry from Jersey City. Old Mr. Schrum, an art dealer, told me of a rich man in Newark who wanted a miniature of his daughter painted. I went to see him and showed him some of my work. When I told him the price would be fifty dollars, he laughed at me. He said a painting twenty times the size would cost him only eight dollars.

"I had just enough money to buy my ferry ticket back to New York. I felt as if I didn't want to live another day. I must have looked as I felt, for I saw *him* on the row of seats opposite me, looking at me as if he understood. He was nice looking, but, oh, above everything else, he looked kind. When one is tired or unhappy or hopeless, kindness counts more than anything else.

"When I got so miserable that I couldn't fight against it any longer, I got up and walked slowly out the rear door of the ferryboat cabin. No one was there, so I climbed quickly over the rail and dropped into the water. Oh, friend Hetty, it was cold, cold!

"For just one moment I wished I was back in the old Vallambrosa, starving and hoping. And then I got numb and didn't care. And then I felt that somebody else was in the water close by me, holding me up. He had followed me, and jumped in to save me.

"Somebody threw a thing like a big, white doughnut at us, and he made me put my arms through the hole. Then the ferryboat backed up, and they pulled us on board. Oh, Hetty, I was so ashamed of my wickedness in trying to drown myself. Besides, my hair had all tumbled down and was sopping wet, and I looked just terrible!

"And then some men in blue clothes came around. *He* gave them his card, and I heard him tell them he had seen me drop my purse on the edge of the boat outside the rail, and in leaning over to get it I had fallen overboard. Then I remembered having read in the papers that people who try to kill themselves are locked up in cells with people who try to kill other people, and I was afraid.

"But some ladies on the boat took me downstairs to the furnace room and got me nearly dry and did up my hair. When the boat landed, *he* came and put me in a cab. He was all dripping himself, but laughed as if he thought it was all a joke. He begged me, but I wouldn't tell him my name or where I lived, I was so ashamed."

"You were a fool, child," said Hetty, kindly. "Wait till I turn the light up a bit. I wish to Heaven we had an onion."

"Then he raised his hat," went on Cecilia, "and said: 'All right. But I'll find you, anyhow. I'm going to claim my rights of salvage.'[15] Then he gave money to the cab driver and told him to take me where I wanted to go, and walked away. What is 'salvage,' Hetty?"

"The edge of a piece of fabric that ain't hemmed or sewn,"[16] said the shopgirl. "You must have looked pretty frazzled to the little hero boy."

"It's been three days," moaned the miniature painter, "and he hasn't found me yet."

---

[15] claim my rights of salvage—take what one has pulled out of the water or up from the bottom of the sea.

[16] Hetty is talking about *selvage*, not salvage.

"Give him a little more time," said Hetty. "This is a big town. Think of how many girls he might have to see soaked in water with their hair down before he would recognize you. The stew's getting on fine— but, oh, for an onion! I'd even use a piece of garlic if I had it."

The beef and potatoes bubbled merrily, giving out a mouth-watering fragrance that even so seemed to lack something—just one more ingredient.

"I came near drowning in that awful river," said Cecilia, shuddering.

"It ought to have more water in it," said Hetty. "The stew, I mean. I'll go get some at the sink."

"It smells good," said the artist.

"That nasty old North River?" objected Hetty. "It smells to me like soap factories and wet dogs— oh, you mean the stew. Well, I wish we had an onion for it. Did he look like he had money?"

"First he looked kind," said Cecilia. "I'm sure he was rich; but that matters so little. When he took out his wallet to pay the cabman, you couldn't help seeing hundreds and thousands of dollars in it. And I looked over the cab doors and saw him leave the ferry station in a motor car. The driver gave him a fur blanket, for he was sopping wet. And it was only three days ago."

"What a fool!" said Hetty, shortly.

"Oh, the driver wasn't wet," breathed Cecilia. "And he drove the car away very nicely."

In his hand he bore an onion—a pink, smooth, solid, shining onion, as large around as a ninety-eight-cent alarm clock.

"I mean *you*," said Hetty. "For not giving him your address."

"I never give my address to drivers," said Cecilia, proudly.

"I wish we had one," said Hetty, unhappily.

"What for?"

"For the stew, of course—Oh, I mean an onion." Hetty took a pitcher and started to the sink at the end of the hall.

A young man came down the stairs from above just as she was opposite the lower step. He was decently dressed, but pale and **haggard**.[17] His eyes were dull with the stress of some physical or mental unhappiness. In his hand he bore an onion—a pink, smooth, solid, shining onion, as large around as a ninety-eight-cent alarm clock.

---

[17] **haggard**—very tired.

Hetty stopped. So did the young man. There was something Joan of Arc-ish and Herculean in her expression at that moment. She had given up the roles of Job and Little Red Riding Hood. The young man stopped at the foot of the stairs and coughed. He felt marooned, held up, attacked, caught, trapped, **sacked**,[18] even browbeaten,[19] although he had no idea why. It was the look in Hetty's eyes that did it. In them he saw a pirate's joy, although he had no idea that the cargo he carried was the thing that was causing such joy.

"Beg your pardon," said Hetty, as sweetly as her harsh voice permitted, "but did you find that onion on the stairs? There was a hole in my paper bag; and I've just come out to look for it."

The young man coughed for half a minute. That moment may have given him the courage to defend his own property. He clutched his onion even more tightly and said in a hoarse voice, "No, I didn't find it on the stairs. It was given to me by Jack Bevens, on the top floor. If you don't believe it, ask him. I'll wait until you do."

"I know about Bevens," said Hetty, sourly. "He writes books and things up there that end up in the

---

[18] **sacked**—defeated.
[19] browbeaten—intimidated; bullied.

trash after a month or so. Say—do you live in the Vallambrosa?"

"I do not," said the young man. "I come to see Bevens sometimes. He's my friend. I live two blocks west."

"What are you going to do with the onion?—If you don't mind my asking," said Hetty.

"I'm going to eat it."

"Raw?"

"Yes, as soon as I get home."

"Haven't you got anything else to eat with it?"

The young man thought briefly.

"No," he confessed. "Where I live, there's not another scrap of anything to eat. I think old Jack Bevens is pretty hard up for grub[20] in his house, too. He hated to give up the onion, but I pestered him until he let me have it."

"Mister," said Hetty, fixing him with her world-knowing eyes and laying a bony but impressive finger on his sleeve, "You've known trouble, too, haven't you?"

"Lots," said the onion owner quickly. "But this onion is my own property, honestly come by. If you will excuse me, I must be going."

"Listen," said Hetty, growing whiter with anxiety. "Raw onion is a mighty poor diet. And so is a beef

---

[20] grub—food.

stew without one. Now, if you're Jack Bevens' friend, I guess you're probably an honest man. There's a little lady—a friend of mine—in my room there at the end of the hall. Both of us are out of luck, and we had just potatoes and meat between us. They're stewing now. But the stew, it ain't got any soul. There's something lacking to it. There's certain things in life that are naturally intended to fit and belong together. One is a pink tablecloth and green roses, and one is ham and eggs, and the other is toddlers and trouble. And the other one is beef and potatoes *with* onions. And still another one is people who are up against it and other people who are in the same kind of trouble."

The young man went into a long attack of coughing. With one hand, he hugged his onion to his chest.

"That's true, that's true," said he, eventually. "But, as I said, I must be going because—"

Hetty grabbed onto his sleeve.

"Don't be an idiot, Little Brother. Don't eat raw onions. Give it to me, and you'll have a dinner of the best stew you ever licked a spoon over. Must two ladies knock a young gentleman down and drag him inside just to get him to dine with them? No harm will come to you, Little Brother. Loosen up and fall into line."

The young man's pale face relaxed into a grin.

"I believe I'll go with you," he said, brightening. "If my onion is good as a **credential**,[21] I accept the invitation gladly."

"It's good as that, but it's better as seasoning," said Hetty. "You come and stand outside the door until I ask my lady friend if she has any objections. And don't run away with that onion before I come out."

Hetty went into her room and closed the door. The young man waited outside.

"Cecilia, kid," said the shopgirl, oiling the sharp saw of her voice as well as she could, "there's an onion outside—with a young man attached. I've asked him in to dinner. You ain't going to mind, are you?"

"Oh, dear!" said Cecilia, sitting up and patting her artistic hair. She cast a sad glance at the ferry-boat poster on the wall.

"Silly," said Hetty. "It ain't him. This is real life now. I believe you said your hero friend had money and automobiles. This is a poor guy who's got nothing to eat but an onion. But he's nice and not pushy, and we need the onion. Shall I bring him in? I'll guarantee his behavior."

---

[21] **credential**—something that gives confidence to help a person be accepted.

"Hetty, dear," sighed Cecilia, "I'm so hungry. What difference does it make whether he's a prince or a burglar? I don't care. Bring him in if he's got anything to eat with him."

Hetty went back into the hall. The onion man was gone. Her heart missed a beat, and a gray look settled over her face except on her nose and cheek-bones. And then the blood flowed again, for she saw the man leaning out the front window at the other end of the hall. She hurried there. He was shouting to some one below. The noise of the street was louder than the sound of her footsteps. She looked down over his shoulder, saw whom he was speaking to, and heard his words. He pulled himself in from the window sill and saw her standing over him.

"I'm so hungry. What difference does it make whether he's a prince or a burglar?"

Hetty's eyes bored into him like two steel spikes.

"Don't lie to me," she said, calmly. "What were you going to do with that onion?"

The young man covered a cough and faced her with an honest look.

"I was going to eat it," said he, slowly, "just as I told you before."

"And you have nothing else to eat at home?"

"Not a thing."

"What kind of work do you do?"

"I am not working at anything just now."

"Then why," said Hetty, with her voice set on its sharpest edge, "do you lean out of windows and give orders to drivers in green automobiles in the street below?"

"Then why," asked Hetty, never giving up, "why were you going to eat a raw onion?"

The young man flushed, and his dull eyes began to sparkle.

"Because, madam," said he, speaking faster and faster, "I pay the driver's wages and I own the automobile—and also this onion—this onion, madam."

He waved the onion within an inch of Hetty's nose. But the brave shopgirl did not move back even a hair.

"Then why do you eat onions," she said, with biting **contempt**,[22] "and nothing else?"

"I never said I did," retorted the young man. "I said I had nothing else to eat where I live. I do not live in a delicatessen."[23]

"Then why," asked Hetty, never giving up, "why were you going to eat a raw onion?"

"My mother," said the young man, "always made me eat a raw onion for a cold. You may have noticed

---

[22] **contempt**—lack of respect.

[23] delicatessen—store that sells meats and cheeses.

that I have a very, very bad cold. I was going to eat the onion and go to bed. I wonder why I am standing here and saying I'm sorry to you for it."

"How did you catch this cold?" went on Hetty, suspiciously.

The young man seemed to have reached an extreme height of feeling. There were two ways he could come down—anger or laughter. He chose wisely, and the empty hall echoed with his hoarse laughter.

"You're great," said he. "And I don't blame you for being careful. I don't mind telling you. I got wet. I was on a North River ferry a few days ago when a girl jumped overboard. Of course, I—"

Hetty extended her hand, stopping his story.

"Give me the onion," she said.

The young man set his jaw a trifle harder.

"Give me the onion," she repeated.

He grinned, and laid it in her hand.

Then Hetty's grim, sad smile showed itself. She took the young man's arm and pointed with her other hand to the door of her room.

"Little Brother," she said, "go in there. The little fool you fished out of the river is there waiting for you. Go on in. I'll give you three minutes before I come. Potatoes is in there, waiting. Go on in, Onions."

After he had tapped at the door and entered, Hetty began to peel and wash the onion at the sink. She gave a gray look at the gray roofs outside, and the smile on her face vanished by little jerks and twitches.

"But it's me," she said, grimly, to herself, "it's me that furnished the beef."

THE END